Subtle Man Loses His Day Job
and Other Stories

Subtle Man Loses His Day Job and Other Stories

by

THOMAS ALLBAUGH

RESOURCE *Publications* • Eugene, Oregon

SUBTLE MAN LOSES HIS DAY JOB AND OTHER STORIES

Resource Publications
An Imprint of Wipf and Stock Publishers
199 W. 8th Ave., Suite 3
Eugene, OR 97401

www.wipfandstock.com

PAPERBACK ISBN: 978-1-7252-5937-9
HARDCOVER ISBN: 978-1-7252-5938-6
EBOOK ISBN: 978-1-7252-5939-3

Manufactured in the U.S.A.   SEPTEMBER 11, 2020

For Cathy

"Nevertheless there still exist towns and countries where people have now and then an inkling of something different. In general it doesn't change their lives. Still, they have had an intimation, and that's so much to the good."

Albert Camus, *The Plague*

Contents

Side Step Is Mainstream

Technically, it began with the bet.
But that's technically. To my mind—and I think I ought to know—it all really started with the preacher. On a hot, cloudless night last summer, when Mike had the air on, and everyone's thoughts were on the fine things in life, the door opened and this short, thin fella walked in with a tennis racket and a raincoat. Now, like I've said many times before, we're not one extreme or another, so puritan types never bother us. Occasionally you overhear a relative in drinking soda with one of the regulars, trying to get him churched, but that's always just sort of fun, gives us something to talk about after the relative goes home. But this time, it was, well, I think the word is incongruous.

First thing, he walked up to my girlfriend Marilyn working behind the bar at the time, and she saw the black raincoat—too hot for a night like this one, not to mention there wasn't rain, not even in the forecast—and she smiled and said in that mocking tone she can use so well, "What's your pleasure, Noah?"

Well, he stood there, all five feet of him, oblivious to insult, looked into her eyes, and said, "Marilyn."

Her mocking look melted because he had said her name, and I mean her mind just kind of got carried away from the bar there and out into the streets and beyond until she was remembering being a girl in high school before her parents had to sell their house in the suburbs. I'd never seen that look in her eyes before. She looked at him again and said, in this gentle voice, "Do I know you?"

"God does."

Now, let me tell you, for years Side Step has been my place of refuge. It's in just the right place, far enough away from the night strip where the prostitutes hang out close to the State Capitol so we don't get bothered by reformers, but still far enough away from the east side of town and the university, so we don't have to put up with droves of first-time drunks puking up Tom Collins. In a word, Side Step is mainstream. Mike, the owner, has helped so many people that I stopped counting, and they all come in and share a cold one and a game of pool and tell you so. I'm not saying it's heaven. But he took in old Cheney after his own bar went bust. Cheney had sipped himself via martinis into invalid status, when Mike goes and takes him in, and lets him retire in the apartment over Side Step, which really makes me mad when I think about it. Helmut, too. He came after he got out of prison, and Side Step gave him a real good place to mend and get back into things. Mike let him work a little, but he really watched him, and it really gets me when I think about what happened on account of what I think you could call a religious extremist.

So he says that to Marilyn about God, and I thought, here we go with the latest. You always see the latest on those televangelist shows with the ugly settings and the phone number you can call to give money. Well, for Marilyn, a strange new distraction came into her face. Before he left, this short fellow gave her a card and talked with her. I'll tell you I was bothered all night because of that, because of how it seemed miraculous the way he said her name. But there's always an explanation.

And it came on the following Wednesday night when I was in, sharing a few with Phil and Dean. Marilyn came up and Dean said, "You see your friend in yet tonight?"

"Friend?"

"Recreation Man. Came in yesterday with a volleyball."

Marilyn said, "Why should he be my friend?"

"He gave you his card," said Dean.

"He's a friend to all," said Phil.

"What's he doing here?" Dean asked.

"What are you doing here?" Marilyn asked.

"Solving the world's problems," said Phil.

"So is he," said Marilyn.

"Oh, take a joke."

Just as Phil said this, the door opened to the brightness outside, throwing into dark silhouette the pool players inside, and in walked Rec Man with his tennis racket again. This time, he was minus the raincoat.

Marilyn watched him while we all sort of frowned and studied our drinks. Then she stepped to the bar, which was only a few feet from the booth we always occupied, and asked, "What do you need?"

"Just here to see Frank," he said. Then he sat down with Frank there at the bar.

Cheney, on his bar stool next to Frank, said, "He your tennis partner?"

"He's a friend." So here was my answer. Not only about why this guy was here in the first place, that is, to see Frank Spilli, who had been on the mend for a while in one of this guy's church programs. Apparently, Recreation Man had come looking for him again. But that also explained how it was that Rec Man knew Marilyn's name—Frank had told him.

"Hey, it's Rec Man," came a shout from Helmut at the pool table. Helmut lifts weights and always wears sleeveless shirts in summer. He's a little younger than the rest of us. He's got one of those silly, thin, blonde mustaches. Well, I thought he stared at Rec Man a little too long, and I felt trouble, because, as I said already, Helmut had done time.

But Dean, from our booth, said, "Do you represent some new type of recreation club?"

"It's funny you put it that way," Rec Man said. "Recreation is such an interesting word. It means literally to create again. It also means a kind of restful activity in our leisure hours. It is rest and, yet, re-creation. How is that possible—I mean resting and re-creating?"

Dean stared his blankest stare.

"Re-creation happens in the saving work of Christ," Rec Man said. "He loves to bring people into his eternal re-creation."

Dean wrinkled his nose like he really disagreed, but Phil raised his glass up into Rec Man's face and said, "Name your poison."

"A damn Sunday school lesson," Cheney coughed, "a damn Sunday school lesson," then stood up, wavering, his thin frame stopped there on the floor. It's one of the seven wonders of the modern world that he can even stand up. Anyway, "Who didn't pay their tithes?" he shouted. "Who brought the preacher looking in here?"

Then he stumbled somehow toward the facilities.

"What are you bothering old bums for?" Dean said.

"Cheney is not an old bum," Marilyn said, and I smelled danger. I mean, she had studied social work in the eighties before dropping out and giving up on the thing, so I could understand that she had compassion. But here she was, defending Rec Man, who next said, "Jesus loves you. All of us." The thing is, you see, that he didn't really shout it. He said it in this quiet way, almost as though he weren't really saying it.

"Get him out of here," Cheney growled from the bathroom doorway. "I pay my tab."

"No, you don't," Marilyn said. Then, to Rec Man, she said, "Look, I understand your wanting to help, but. . ." and didn't finish.

Rec Man had picked up his racket, placed his card and some phone change in front of Frank. "Call me any time, day or night." Then he walked out.

Then the rain began.

Cheney, back at the bar doing Jack Daniels, said to Marilyn, sort of in the way Dean asked, "Your friend coming in anymore tonight?"

I'm sure that the rain reminded him of Rec Man, coming down on the sidewalk outside, where we heard it, through the open door, slapping the sidewalk, the wet reflecting the neon lights. To be honest, the rain, the way it came, just unsettled me.

I was still sitting with Dean and Phil, and we were on a pitcher. "I used to be a Christian," I admitted.

"Every red-blooded American is a Christian," Helmut said.

"No, they aren't," I said.

"Oh, not this again," Cheney said.

Marilyn sat down next to me. There was fatigue in her eyes. In a tone of voice that betrayed sadness, she said, "Everyone is so stuck all the time."

"I'm not stuck," Dean objected.

"I wish that God called my name," I said.

"Do you?" Dean asked. "I mean, do you really want to have your free choice smashed in just like that?"

I ducked into my beer. He had a point.

Over at the dart board, Bill Eschavaria, who works at Chrysler, said in the most exaggerated way, sounding like Billy Graham, "And that, brethren, is faith," threw a dart, and missed completely. Then he came up to the bar. "I want to let you in on what happened to me last summer," he said looking from Marilyn to Cheney at the bar. "Something profound that I've never been able to explain rationally."

"If you can explain it," I said, "aren't you using rationality?"

"No, no, no. Now. I was just discussing the boulder on the corner of City High School. It's been there a long time, hasn't it?" He looked at Cheney.

"Not as square as it once was, but it's always been there," Cheney said.

"Well, I say I saw rocks like that in Wyoming last summer. No, listen. I saw them changed in an instant into grown men." I couldn't believe how stupid it was. I haven't thought well of Eschavaria since.

Cheney just started to cough.

Bill raised his hand. "I saw it happen."

"When did you go to Wyoming?" Helmut asked.

"This is stupid," I said. "Maybe it's time to call it a night."

"I'll place five hundred on it," said Eschavaria.

I mumbled, but then began to say clearly, "People only believe what they see. An unbelieving generation demands a sign. But no sign shall be given it except the sign of Jonah."

"Noah," said Helmut.

"No, it's Jonah," I said. "I know. It wouldn't make any sense if it were Noah."

Helmut shrugged. "I don't see the difference."

"Yes," Bill said, "we all know bits of the Bible here. But I saw it. And I'm willing to wager that rock at the corner of City School is one of them."

"I'll tell you about unbelieving generations," Cheney said. "1939, Nazi Germany building up troops to invade Poland. Couldn't accept that Hitler meant to do it. So, 1941, men like me walking over Europe. Only us and the English stopped him."

"You tell him, Cheney," Helmut yelled.

"Then you don't believe," said Bill.

Cheney moved his jaw to speak but could only hack and cough.

"Then you will place a bet with Marilyn here, that the City School rock will not change into a man come tomorrow morning?"

"Not on your life."

"You must really believe me then. Just as I thought. You are hiding."

"Oh, I'll wager five thousand," Cheney said, his throat finally clear. "I'll enjoy the money, too. Maybe reopen my business."

Bill shook his hand. "It is a bet." And then he walked out. I don't know what he was thinking—maybe that Cheney was too drunk to remember shaking on it.

Helmut came around to where Cheney was smoking a Camel. "I'll bet Eschavaria is going to take that rock off school property and try to say that it turned into a man, unless we can get there first."

Cheney scowled.

"I could come around with my brother's pickup. He'll let me use it if I give him a good enough reason."

"Good enough reason, Helmut, come on," said Marilyn.

"Five thousand greenbacks is a good reason. I could get some help, too."

"Another chance to show off the training, Helmut?" Marilyn asked. "Eschavaria hasn't got five thousand dollars."

"I don't need to prove anything."

"Besides," I said, "aren't you still on probation?"

He drank his Milwaukee's finest.

"Look," said Marilyn, "if you tried to remove it, Eschavaria would say it really did change or some such nonsense."

Helmut seemed not to hear or understand her.

"Martin," Cheney said, "You used to be in the service."

"My name's not Martin," I said. "It's Martyr."

"What?" Cheney said.

"Martyr. Martyr Alexander."

"Your mother hate you or something?"

"Moment of inspiration."

Now usually Marilyn would say at this point, "Whyn't you go by Alex?" This was one of our subjects. But on this night she didn't, I noticed, as I saw that Helmut had finished his beer and was walking out the door.

"Coulda been worse," I said to fill the gap. "I could've been Caesar Martyr."

No one laughed.

Anyway, after the Side Step closed that night we ate breakfast at Denny's, our usual place. On this night a cop was sitting down the counter from us, and the waitress had just brought our eggs when we heard on his beeper something about vandals at City High School.

After the cop left, we went over in Marilyn's 1979 Lincoln. It was still raining, but we drove around the high school, keeping away from the two cop cars that threw their disturbing blues and reds over the trees and the houses across the street. Finally we inched toward the spot, the wipers going full blast, and sure enough, the rock that had stood at the corner for generations, but had been leaning a little of late and wasn't as square as it used to be, was gone.

In the morning I went over to have coffee at the Side Step. Mike was at the bar and said, "What's your take on what happened here last night?"

I told him.

Mike said, "So you think it's Helmut?"

"Helmut? What's he done?"

"Come with me upstairs." We went to the back parking lot and up the wooden steps leading to the apartment, and those steps were muddied and some of them freshly chewed up at the edges. We went upstairs into the apartment and there was the huge, jagged shape of the City High School boulder muddying the floor next to the bed where Cheney slept. Somehow sensing our movement, Cheney sat up in his alcoholic haze, turned, looked squarely at the rock, as though to make sure that the rock had not been transformed into a man, and then rolled back over to sleep. There were also ropes tied tightly around the rock and then wrapped around his covered, thin body. The rock itself was taller than Cheney and many times his width.

Back in the bar, I said to Mike, "Well, in so many words I've told you what I really think. Helmut was just an accomplice."

Mike stared out the window and the police radio he had dragged in was on behind the bar, and I felt real bad for him, because as I've said already, this is the trash you always get for helping people out.

"You going to press charges against him?" I asked.

"I'll tell you what we're lookin' at. Closing the bar down. . ."

"No."

"Or covering up. I'll tell you, Marty, I've had enough trouble with the public because of the people I've helped."

"I guess you know," I said.

"Helmut has no idea of the trouble he's caused me. No idea."

Mike was taking it real personal-like. "He's a pawn," I said. "Just a pawn."

Well, Mike had the boys come over and start to pulverize the boulder. It took more than that night, though, and let me tell you it sent the fear of God into all of us sitting down below there in that bar while we knew the chiseling was going on upstairs.

Anyway, the next night, who should innocently show up but Rec Man, in the rain coat again with his racket. Well, we had had enough tension in two nights to last one week, or at least I had, and I was certain that he was the reason that Mike might be closing down, and I wasn't going to stand for it. This was when I realized that Marilyn didn't feel the same way.

In he came, sat down and asked for Frank again. None of us had seen him or Eschavaria—or Helmut.

"Look," Marilyn began, "I respect what you're about, trying to help people and set a good example and all. But I'm not sure that you understand the people who come in places like this enough to help them. You may just push them over the edge."

"In fact you *have* pushed them over the edge," I said, coming over now beside him from Dean and Phil's table.

"Marty," said Marilyn.

But Rec Man was calm. "In places like this my faith began." And he looked in my eyes with his brokenness.

I had balled up my fist and stared him in those pale blue eyes, waiting for them to go bloodshot with fear and then look away, and then I was going to pound him into the bar.

"Your faith began in a bar?" Marilyn asked. Then she turned to me. "It won't do any good, Marty."

"Yes, it will," I said, understating like Clint Eastwood, letting my eyes do the talking.

But he looked like he was just a pair of eyes staring through a head in a body that was dead and gone and had no more use for pain or pleasure. I hadn't seen that look for at least fifteen years, and I had forgotten that it existed, that there really were people in the world broken and healed by Jesus. And he seemed enveloped in something. I've never told Marilyn that, never admitted it. But it was as though he were protected.

Marilyn said, "Marty, you will get the cops in here." She glanced upstairs. "That's not something I think you want to do tonight."

Oblivious to everything, Rec Boy said, "It was in a place like this I used to spend my paycheck. Talking to the other drunks, I was always surprised at how many customers had religion relics in their background, an experience of heaven, an idea of God, but thrown away for the pursuit of some other thing." He said this looking at me, not at Marilyn. "It's almost as though every action of theirs was settled into the direction of trying to prove that He doesn't exist. Or, that there are many other possibilities, because if you can prove that, then the gospel accounts were somehow wrong, and you could go your own way. Just so long as there isn't just one way, like the gospel says."

Dean had come up on his other side, and he pointed at him and said, "Virtue does not exist. It is only the authorities scaring citizens into compliance."

"Yes," Rec Boy said. "Except that you've really only demonstrated original sin and humanity's need for God's grace."

That's the problem, I thought. That's really the problem. And you never quite get away from it.

One week later, the rock had finally been sent out in bits, when I could swear a whole fleet of cop cars came and blocked off the parking lot when they apprehended Helmut for going out of state and breaking his probation. I couldn't believe it. All for a stupid rock, one that had been falling over on the school grounds and no one had even bothered to straighten. But they never found anything, no evidence. Mike handled the cops' questions with his usual aplomb, I believe the word is, never blinking, always ready to help the young officers. And then it blew over.

Now Eschavaria, if he's drunk and Mike isn't in, will assert his claim. Cheney will demand the five thousand dollar payment. And in spite of how calm Mike was that night when the cops came in, he tells me that he dreams some nights that some young detective has come into the bar with a chip of the rock and asks to look upstairs. Mike dreams that the detective will see parts of the wooden stairs that are chewed up, and will pretend like Columbo to believe that the marks on the wooden stairs really did come from the new refrigerator Mike put in for Cheney to cover for the rock being moved up there. In a way, the rock still haunts Side Step.

No, I'll tell you, Side Step is mainstream. But people are always going off one end or another. It happens all the time with religion and politics. It almost seems like there is no mainstream any more. Only people out on trips.

Transistor Radio

A Story of Love and Technology

The winter Dad left, taking the hi-fi with him, I discovered the easy, unconditional love of the transistor radio. With earplug inserted, the radio under my covers, and my face turned to the wall, I could appear to be asleep when Mom looked in. After she closed the door, I would listen long into the night to the stream coming from beyond where the city lay. From night to night, the rankings of songs might change, but Stevie Wonder's "Signed, Sealed, and Delivered" started to climb, though hearing it usually took waiting through "Bridge Over Troubled Waters"—a tedious imitation of classical music, I thought, especially when you knew the real thing—or "Let It Be." This song, like "Bridge," stayed at number one entirely too long that early spring. I suppose my being Catholic made it mandatory that I tolerate it. But we listened to better Beatles songs in art class.

Mostly, if I tuned in long enough, the songs would come around again. But with the radio, there was always that feeling that I was about to hear something new. After a month or so, of course, waiting for my favorite song wasn't enough to keep me awake, and I found myself starting to drift off only to wake up to the guitar solo in "Light My Fire" or the new version of "In-A-Gadda Da Vida," with its faster beat and its longer solos. Late, after midnight, the DJ played longer and more obscure stuff—I'd imagine him sleeping or taking long cigarette breaks. One night I awoke to the sound of a scratched Door's tune jumping over and over again, as though Jim Morrison had the hiccups. "I am the Lizard K—Lizard K—Lizard K—Lizard K—Lizard K. . ." I snapped off my radio, set it on my desk, and went to sleep.

Before Dad left, I used to listen to classical music on the stereo. I struggled through violin lessons and went to concerts of Shostakovich symphonies and Brahms overtures, Mozart marches and Beethoven concertos. I listened to classical music instead of the Monkees, The Turtles, Strawberry Alarm Clock, and Donovan. At sock hops held over the noon hour in the gym, I stood along the side while the girls danced in their stockings to "Dizzy," Frigid Pink's electric, heavy version of "House of the Rising Sun," and then Gary Puckett & the Union Gap's "Woman." I loved watching them dance even as I sensed the lack of talent in the recording artists I was hearing.

Then the day came when Nick Carlson, from next door, invited me to hear his band play. He had put together a band that included three of the Sanchez kids, who were new to the school. Nick told me that they were going to play before a party in the Sanchez's' basement. The Sanchez family had recently moved to a house just down the street from school. This was about five blocks from where we lived, but Nick Carlson's family seemed a lot like the Sanchez family in that they appeared to be better off than my family. Nick was the oldest of three. His dad was a successful boat salesman, and Nick got everything. He had gotten a pinball machine in his basement for his tenth birthday. In sixth grade, Nick received an electric guitar, guitar lessons, a four-track tape deck, and an entire PA system for Christmas. The year I was listening to my transistor radio long into the night, Nick's family had removed the big tree from the middle of their backyard. This was apparently one of their first steps towards putting in a new swimming pool.

Nick's band played through his PA system. Nick played a Les Paul guitar, while Dave Van Horn was on a Fender bass. The Sanchez kids contributed the other instruments, with the older brother Tom on the drums, the younger brother Vince on rhythm guitar, and their sister Carmina on tambourine. The Sanchez's had moved to town the previous summer from Texas, and their father was some sort of executive for a firm. I still don't remember how I came to be invited to this event. Both Nick and the Sanchez's were moving in opposite directions from me and my family. They were building swimming pools in their backyards and getting electric guitars for their birthdays, while my family needed rides to the grocery store. But that night, I was one of them, and their sound was huge, not as in big, but as in "This is an event." This was new. This was what changed and moved things. This was rock and roll.

Because I played violin in orchestra, or perhaps I had some ability with music (I had been tested for it in fourth grade, and that's when I was given the violin to play), I was able to follow this. Each player was doing his part. The drums kicked in, and Nick and Dave laid down the first guitar and bass riff of The Beatles' "Birthday." Nick did a good Paul McCartney vocal, while Carmina and her brothers echoed back to him. And when the short drum solo-rev up came, and Carmina added the tambourine, I felt the foundations of my being churning in the renewing chaos.

Afterwards, the silence like the emptiness after blasted walls of buildings, I fell in with the strange bored talk as the band agreed that the song was okay, except for one turn where they moved into the last verse. So they were taking it up again from that point. I hadn't noticed any mistake and was grateful to have the earthquake of the guitar, drums, and bass again. I could have heard it all night.

When they turned off the amps, I walked over and stood next to Carmina. I understood that I was momentarily in a position of privilege. "That was. . .good," I said.

"Thanks." She slouched on her right leg, her left foot in pointed black shoes aimed at me, her left knee bent. Though she had not developed curves yet, her legs were wonderfully shaped and slender from playing in sports.

"I mean it. That was great."

She just nodded.

Standing next to her for the first time, seeing the deep brown strands of her hair parted across her olive forehead and her retainer against her close, full front teeth, I wanted to tell her how great her band was. I wanted to lie, to tell her that I played something cool like the guitar.

"Mike plays the violin," Nick said. He was across the room, unplugging the PA system.

Carmina looked up then, as if noticing me for the first time. "Really?"

I wanted to deny this. I wanted to run. As always, my failures to meet the criteria set by my peer group were made crystal clear.

"Well," I said, "I sorta used to." This was as true as I could make it.

Nick looped a microphone cord neatly around his hand and elbow. "We should have him help us with some Emerson, Lake & Palmer. Or the Moody Blues. You know them, right Mike?"

I smiled. "Yes." I had never heard of Emerson, Lake & Palmer. Or the Moody Blues. Neither had been on late-night transistor radio.

Even with the loss of our stereo and the car, which Dad had taken because he said he had to work, I had been okay. I had compensated. But clearly, now, I had missed too much being in orchestra and attending concerts with the local symphony. In fifth grade, for my birthday, I'd heard the local symphony play the Brahms fourth, and I had been so haunted that I'd found a copy in the K-Mart records department and gotten it for a few dollars. Sitting in the dark hall and listening to music that had been written so long ago that was so rich, my mind had opened to all of the weather and nature out of reach beyond our city of sewers and sidewalks. Most of the time, the stereo was my refuge, and for three summers I'd checked out records from the local library and got to know all of the major works of the major composers.

Now, I had the transistor radio, and the tiny, static-filled music came through as a shrill representation that I could always hold at a distance. Even the recordings played at sock hops seemed trite. But now, after that night, hearing Nick and the Sanchez family play, this was what could not be denied. After that night, prodded by the fact that I'd never heard of Emerson, Lake & Palmer or the

Moody Blues, I began to use my transistor radio as a data stream, especially if the DJ talked. In the weeks that followed, I was the only one in the eighth grade, I found out, who liked for the DJs to talk. So when "Mellow Yellow" came on and the DJ told me exactly which year it had been a hit, I saw this as important information. It didn't seem like enough, if I was going to make up for my classical music past, to just know the artist. I needed excess information that would allow me a certain comfortable margin should music come up in conversation. I needed to say, "Oh, but 'I'm a Believer' wasn't even written by The Monkees. The composer was Neil Diamond." Or, as the DJ had said one night, "Yeah, 'Summer in the City' sure captured 1968, and John Sebastian should have stayed with them."

Carmina didn't say hi to me in the hallways between classes, but after a month of hearing "Bridge Over Troubled Waters" way too many times, and "Signed, Sealed, and Delivered" was starting to peak, I decided to ask her to be my partner for coed doubles in the school ping pong tournament. She said yes, and days later, I was back in Carmina's basement after school. Her brother's drum set was in the corner next to an amp and Nick's PA system. The ping pong table was up, and we played for a while with her mother watching us and asking me questions about my family. I was happy to have her mother there. She was still attractive, still thin even though she'd had four children. She dressed well, even at home, like one of my teachers. Something about being included in Carmina's family left me feeling fuller than I did at home, and I told her that my dad had met someone else and my mom had kicked him out. When I talked about my family, Mrs. Sanchez would listen sympathetically, and she asked how it was that my father had gotten to take the stereo. "It seems like he would have to wait for the courts to decide that," she said.

"Really?" I asked.

Carmina simply waited on the other end for me to serve the ball again. When I did, I didn't say anything more and concentrated on the volley. I had to admit that with things as they stood now, I didn't really miss the stereo. Things were fine. All we had were records like Rubinstein's version of Beethoven's Fifth Piano Concerto or Van Cliburn playing Tchaikovsky and Rachmaninov concertos. Dad had apparently left these because they reminded him too much of my mom and our family. There in the basement with the drum set in the corner, this was not imagery that I even wanted in my mind as I talked to Mrs. Sanchez and her lovely, though still very thin and small Carmina. I wanted them to know that I had fully arrived for them. I wanted them to know that I had always been who they were seeing now, in this moment. No other moments mattered.

After ping pong, we went up and played basketball on her family's driveway. Carmina and I were both short but both good ping pong and basketball players. After a few nights of doing this, word got out. When asked, I encouraged it. "Yes, we are partners," I said. "Ping pong partners. Doubles. Coed."

Two days a week, Carmina and I practiced ping pong. Her mother stopped coming down to talk to me or to watch us. Now she left the door to upstairs open, apparently secure that the sound of the ping pong ball would be proof that nothing else was going on. Or Carmina's younger brother would sit next to the table at net level and watch the ball going back and forth. Though he looked bored as we played, he seemed to like me. After a few games, eldest brother and drummer Tom would come home from the high school, and then we would go upstairs and play basketball with her brothers on their shoveled driveway, where the snow banks would keep the ball from going too far out of bounds.

This went on until the day came when her brothers went inside after just one basketball game and Carmina and I were alone.

She held the basketball and wouldn't pass it to me. When I asked for it, she said no and smirked. She crossed her legs like she had to go to the bathroom.

Okay, I thought. This was weird, but my easy attitude held the day. I could go with this. I wasn't new on the scene.

She held the ball out, looked at it, and then cradled it again. "You'll have to come and get it."

This seemed sort of childish. I wasn't about to go over and bat it out of her hands. So I changed the subject. "Do you like Donovan?" I asked.

Carmina shrugged. "No." The most I got out of her that afternoon was that she hated "Let It Be." But suddenly this all seemed unimportant. Even though Carmina's brothers were in a rock band, and she was playing tambourine—even though her family played rock music, she didn't really care. She didn't seem tuned to anything I'd been hearing on my transistor radio. It began to come to me in a dim sort of way that I'd crammed for a test I thought was going to be a certain way, and now it was clear that I was wrong. I was in the presence of the real Carmina, I realized, and I had all this time been responding to an idol.

She dropped the ball then and walked to the edge of the grass where the snow had mostly melted away. She turned her back to me. "I think I have to go in," she said.

That night, I turned the transistor radio on to WGRD and there was no music. Instead, I found I was tuned to a discussion about Lieutenant Calley, who was being tried for war crimes in the My Lai Massacre. Over a hundred Vietnamese civilians were dead. And what Dad had said one night before he left came to me—that in a few years, that would be me in those news films, me lurking in the jungles of Vietnam.

Two days later, the ping pong tournament started. But now, as I stood near Carmina after winning our first two games, her friends came over to us and she would talk to them. I was ignored, but I was ready to forgive her, to overlook the slight. So I assumed it was just a mistake on her part, and I went to her house a day later.

The driveway, the scene of our many basketball games, was empty, clean. The garage door was closed, so I had to knock on the front door. I'd never been to the front door before.

Tom, her older brother, answered, said she wouldn't come out. He told me she didn't think we needed to practice anymore. That was it.

Okay, I said, and turned around and walked away. The thing was, she still had to at least play ping pong with me—that was coming up in five days.

In five days, when we played the next round, she didn't say anything to me. After the games, I hung around near the drinking fountain in the hallway that led to both boys' and girls' locker rooms. No one came out for a long time, though I heard laughter coming from the girls' room. Then some of Carmina's friends, all of whom were also in the tournament, came out with their books, but Carmina wasn't with them. Jan Keely, tall and blonde, who was the center on the girls' basketball team, looked at me and told me that Carmina was with Clifford Merrow.

"He came and got her after your games," Jan said. "I think they went somewhere together."

"They're so cute," Diane Reynolds said.

I hung around the back of the school the next day near the gymnasium until I saw Clifford Merrow talking to her. Clifford, the center on the basketball team, was tall and awkward. Others said their different heights made them a cute couple. But we, Carmina and I, had become all we would ever be—ping pong partners.

We won that year's coed tournament. Our first place award, given at the sports assembly in late May, we received as individuals, standing on opposite sides of our teacher, sort of the way The Beatles were now that their breakup had been announced on the news, and Paul had referred to it as a divorce. At this point, Clifford had also been dumped, it turned out, for the same reason I had been. I learned this at my table in art class.

"Poor Clifford," David Vander Wall said. I didn't ask but leaned in closer as I painted with watercolors and listened as David told the table that Clifford had failed to kiss Carmina.

I looked down at the table. It was probably well known that I also had not done this. I felt real embarrassment then. I was in the growing crowd of those dumped. I was a dumpee. I imagined Clifford facing a similar moment after playing basketball on the driveway with Carmina's brothers, when suddenly the brothers went inside and she waited, waited to be kissed.

What had he done when she stood there coyly in that moment, holding the basketball, not passing it? I had asked her about rock stars. What had Clifford said? We had both been given our moment. We had both failed to kiss Carmina.

I still had the radio under the covers—the all-night repetition of the hit parade, always there, always changing. But I had suddenly become aware that I needed a stereo, because the songs on the radio were not the best songs. I needed to start buying albums. I bought the Moody Blues. I'd heard their song "Question" and couldn't tell what I could do with a violin on it. But there were a few songs with strings on the album.

And then the baseball season arrived, and for a while the games carried me late into the night, and then Dad called and wanted to talk to me about going to the symphony again—just the two of us. I said I would consider it.

Late that summer, after not seeing them or most of my class, I saw the Sanchez family in church. Something about them still drew me. They were a band. They were a family, and their father seemed to laugh with them. Sometimes then, I walked near their house and stood at a distance, watching Carmina playing basketball with her brothers.

I'd go home before I could be seen.

The Lives of the Composers

I am distracted from my beach reading by a pregnant woman in a bikini to my left. She has laid out a blanket, propped up an umbrella with fish neatly drawn on it, and now has placed headphones on the tight, tanned skin of her abdomen. She must be almost full-term. But she is in shape, without fat in her legs, arms, or face. She will lose any baby fat in her stomach after her pregnancy. Under her umbrella alone, she wears ear buds—I assume this is for her own music. The headphones are for her stomach—for her unborn. I have seen this before. She's probably playing Mozart or the Declaration of Independence for her unborn child. Probably she and her husband hope their child becomes a senator someday.

This was really a popular thing to do shortly after my wife and I had our kids, and it really gets me. Recently, some teachers I met in a church program where I was dropping our son off were talking about this, about baby genius and Mozart CDs for the unborn. None of these teachers could pronounce his name, yet they were talking about how to create gifted children. One of them even said "*Bee-th*oven." That's right. "Bee" and "th-."

The pregnant woman coughs, and I shade the sun from my eyes. Would she ever listen to Mozart, or know him from Stravinsky? Her own music has a female vocal over a beat. Probably she would call him "Mosart." Probably claps between movements.

Most Southern Californians treat the concert hall like a Laker game.

Kids walk by with frozen treats and kick a little sand on my blanket. I am shading my eyes, but it's hard to read out here. I am wearing my t-shirt to keep the sun off.

I think about going for a treat, look at the concession stand across the beach through the heat rising from the sand, and close my eyes.

Max started school this week. It's earlier every year. I will try taking him to a concert this year. He's a fifth grader. It's time. That's when I read the lives of the composers. I had a good fifth grade teacher who said *Bay*-toe-ven and MOTE-Zart. The Jupiter Symphony, its dancing first movement, its soaring second movement, its stately, playful minuet, its triumphant finale—I had to hear it every day. I see why people think they will make smart babies.

My parents took me to the symphony. I heard Brahms' Fourth. I found a recording in K-Mart, its sighing and struggling so appropriate to those cloud-filled fall days in the Midwest. I still hear Brahms and think of those days.

I open one eye and study her. She's very pretty, doesn't look like a band geek.

I sit up. She hasn't noticed me. I want to tell her, "Bring the kid to the symphony." In seventh grade, I heard the Shostakovich Fifth—moody cartoon depictions of tyrannical army marches cascading like uncontrolled avalanches over haunting melodies.

"My wife plays the clarinet," I want to say, has had the usual career prescribed by a society convinced that Mozart is valuable for IQs. She has taught music, played for symphony orchestras, community wind ensembles, a ballet troupe, and community theatre pit orchestras, juggled clarinet, flute, sax, and bass clarinet for minimum wage."

I have details like this one my wife taught me because I married her: Mozart, Brahms, and Copeland wrote best for the clarinet. They all had friends who were accomplished clarinetists. Beethoven, she said, did not.

I wish we lived where facts like these mattered.

I stare at the young woman. If she says "Mosart helps kids learn," I will confront her.

Why would she force her child to listen to music she never learned to appreciate? Perhaps the seeds of alienation between mother and child are already being sown.

She takes the headphones from her womb and puts them over her own ears.

Finally, I think, and close my eyes. I hear a wave crash and children scream. Someone strums a guitar. Whimpering comes from nearby. I open my eyes. The pregnant woman is weeping. The headphones are sprawled out in the sand near me. She is hyperventilating.

She is inconsolable.

I sit up and reach over, pick up her headphones in a gesture to give them back. I open them outward so that they are like speakers. As I do, I hear not strains of violins and percussion but a man's voice: "When I return from Afghanistan, I will take you to a Dodgers game. Oh how I miss my Dodgers. Like I miss you."

I reach out to her with the headphones as the voice goes on. It is deep. I look at them. I speak. "Is he—" but don't finish. She turns away. She has been giving her unborn child the voice of the lost father.

Mournful strains from Barber's "Adagio for Strings" appear in my mind. The Adagio is permanently ironed to the 9/11 Twin Towers tragedy through too many YouTube videos so that I can no longer hear it for its universal qualities. Now, the strings of this piece spread out in a whisper of terror's reach in time, even to the unborn, forcing on me the fresh understanding that I haven't really been listening.

Directions from the Hive Mind

When the bee landed on his soda can where he'd placed it on the step to the back parking lot, Richard Martin remembered having bee communication explained in a business class. A bee would return to the hive and dance and turn, and this signified distance and direction. Somehow after the bee danced, more bees would venture out to the source of pollen. Richard could no longer remember the business point being illustrated in this lesson, or whether the turning signified distance or direction. But now, as he peered at his own can of soda and then at the retaining wall of the back parking lot across from him, he thought that the dance was pure and full of the energy of the hive, not drained and overloaded with other systems. There was such fatigue in the world. Imaginations failed. People rarely thought outside of their expectations; they even seemed to fear to do so.

The door behind him scraped open. Jason, in his first year at the local community college, held a box of generic-brand frozen peas. "A customer wants to know if this can be substituted for the sales brand."

Richard shook his head and smiled. "Rain check."

"And Mickey says we need another checkout opened."

"Okay."

Jason turned back, the door slamming shut behind him. Richard had rewarded him last year with the dollar raise. The student was still moving for another. He'd better be careful, Richard thought, dragging heavily again on his cigarette, or he'd wind up with a career in grocery, too.

After one more quick drag, Richard exhaled, tossed the half-burned butt onto the pavement, and entered the store. Passing the break room, he thought of Jason's energy and wondered about himself. What was there to motivate an old man like him? Technically, he wasn't old, not in comparison to most of Europe, he thought, but his thoughts sometimes seemed old. They seemed only negative, only fears—loss of job, loss of health insurance, loss of money for the kids' schools. This must be what it meant to be middle-aged.

He walked by the dairy case and thought of Emilia, his college professor friend. He would see her tomorrow afternoon. As he reached the end of the soap and paper aisle, the registers came into view, all crowded with the carts and the backs of customers leaning in, all of them watching Mickey at the register, making sure that she didn't waste too much of their time and didn't make a mistake. Richard had a momentary thought of the character in a short story set in an A&P store—he had read it in community college English and remembered the narrator getting away at the end, thinking himself to be Queenie's knight in shining armor, only to be hung out to dry in an empty parking lot because she was gone. That character had been a romantic. Richard didn't think himself a romantic. He didn't know what else there was. But he wasn't that.

The light above number 4 blinked two registers down for him, and Beatrice had the phone to her mouth and was again paging for someone to open up a fifth lane. Richard came up and took out his keys, then typed in his code, opened a second express register and stood and waited. The whole thing was deceptive, he thought. There really weren't that many customers in the store. It was just that these customers, trying to be on time for dinner, had all headed for the register at the same time.

Ennui was the word that came to him as he scanned the warm loaf of French bread, a frozen bag of broccoli, two candy bars, and a *National Enquirer* and waited for the customer, a regular, to swipe her store card. He glanced down at his handwritten name tag, a temporary, pinned to his red vest. His official name tag had been missing for the last week and a half. He wondered where he had left it.

How many here, he thought, would suspect the store manager of feeling *ennui*? That was, of course, just his problem, that no one in his workplace would ever know that word. Perhaps only Emilia—he liked to call her that, though she preferred Em. But she could not come here.

After five minutes, the rush was over. Richard walked back again to check on the price of the generic peas, thinking he could make a case for using them. No, it wasn't just fatigue he felt; the most appropriate word really was *ennui*. He wasn't trying to fancy-pants his case. Only this could be that. The cigarette had not stimulated him.

The coffee shop door opened and Emilia walked in carrying a bag with flowers on it. She was about five feet tall, with striking black hair and a delightful nose. Richard was again captured by the way that her diminutive stature seemed to command attention. He did not see their meeting as an affair. He wasn't, after all, motivated by sex so much as companionship, so it couldn't really be adultery, technically. Her faded blue eyes and her straight, Roman nose seemed to be her best features. Her skin was so pale as to suggest weak circulation, especially given her dark hair.

He stood to put his calendar and cell phone in his pocket and then to embrace her, though this time as he stood over her, she did not reciprocate by putting her arms into it.

They sat down.

"I was just about to leave," Richard said. "Or get another coffee. I wasn't sure which."

"Oh." She rubbed her nose. "I had to meet a student who's in danger of failing."

"Yes, of course."

"How was traffic for you?" she asked, looking at his ring finger. He had noticed her doing this the last time. The coffee shop was about thirty minutes from his foothill community.

"Not bad at all," he said. "But then I'm going against the real traffic at this time. You know, have you read Joan Didion?"

She was looking at the menu board. He waited.

"I won't be able to stay long," she said. "Saturday is always better for me."

"Of course." He also wished he could meet with her Saturday, but he would have to take his son with the church youth group to the water amusement park. "As I was saying, my foothill community has been characterized by none other than Joan Didion as a community of hairdressers and Hollywood wannabes—in a word, we're 'outsiders.'" The last was Richard's own inference, but it seemed a sound one. He smiled and Emilia said, "Hm, really. I do like some of Didion."

He watched her place her money on the table and put away her purse.

"But you know, that might just be Joan Didion being snarky again. Someone I know has said that she doesn't really get the Santa Ana winds right. She makes them sound like destruction itself. To me, they're just sort of there."

Richard laughed. "Yes. Exactly. So I don't know. Hey, I posted a review on—"

"Did you now?" She stood and went to the counter. "I've been doing a little online scoping myself of late. Just a minute."

Scoping? He was going to tell her that he had gotten a few comments on his review of the new Jonathan Franzen novel. He realized now in her walking away that it was just an Amazon.com review he had written in his online identity, The Masked Writer.

She returned with a latte and stirred two sugars into it. That seemed entirely too sweet and rich for Richard.

"So," she said, "you were saying. This was your 'Masked Writer' thing."

Something in her inflection on his online *nom de plume* made him wince. "It's just something on Amazon.com."

"No, okay, let's discuss this. Franzen isn't a favorite. But go ahead."

He had listened to her discussion of *Jane Eyre* and her love of gothic and her opinion that everything might be gothic in America at some point, and it had been interesting.

"You know, you might be right," he said, "I mean what you said last week about American Gothic."

"Oh, you think so, do you." It sounded British the way that her question did not resemble the form of a question. She seemed to be playing him.

"Well, yes," he said, "I do." He found his eyes settling on the flavored coffee drink cooling down in front of him as he expected a counterargument or refutation. Instead, she continued to stir her latte.

"You know," she said finally, "I was telling my students today that they are not paying my salary. You know that's what the public all thinks about us, that when they pay their tuition, they are paying our salary. As though they are our boss, as some think with the police force and the fire department. But I told them that no, their tuition payment gives them access. It is access to our services they are buying."

Richard nodded. He was unsure of the direction she was taking this.

"There's a big difference there," she said. "Of course, it's too late to say that this semester. But I'm hoping that by saying this early next semester I'll be able to shift some of my students' attitudes about cutting classes. But I'm sorry to go on about this. You were saying about your review."

"No, nothing."

"Go on."

"Are you okay?" he asked. "I mean. . .you seem. . .like you've had a rotten day or something."

The house had the warm, rich draw of breakfast when Richard walked in, and he thought that perhaps things would still be the same, though he wasn't sure what to make of Emilia's unstable behavior. That was what it had seemed to be. It was unstable. He had sudden doubts that he could trust her.

They had met in a coffee shop where she was serving customers. She was wearing the barista uniform and working, and she had remarked on his Wendell Berry book under his *Inspiring New Employees* handbook for a seminar he was attending that day in Pasadena. Only after a few meetings did Richard learn that she was actually a college professor, and that she had been volunteering to work at the coffee shop in order to avoid being perceived by men as too educated to be desirable. She was truly complex.

He entered the kitchen as Sarah, still in her teaching clothes, removed the last of the bacon from the fat in the pan to the paper toweling on the serving dish. Richard hugged her and remembered the first time he was aware of his teacher's breasts and figure. He was in fifth grade and that was earlier than most of the girls in his class had begun to develop. Sarah had finally been able to teach third grade after seven years at her school, though, so she probably never really had to think about that anymore. Her blouse was unbuttoned at the top in a way that Richard found appealing. He glanced at his ten-year-old son Rudy at the dinner table studying the pasta salad as though it were a foreign substance.

"You're not wearing your wedding band again," Sarah said. "We're not married again."

"Huh? Oh. You know, honey." Her elementary school humor—that the ring was somehow magical and made them married and unmarried, sort of like the hobbit becoming invisible—usually made a joke about it and at the same time allowed him to put it back on.

"I just don't want to catch it on something at work."

"So you always say. You probably lost it."

"None of the managers wear their rings at work. And here it is." He produced it from his pocket.

"What is that?" Rudy asked, sitting at the table.

"What?"

Rudy pointed to the pasta salad. "That."

"Something new," Richard said. "Try it."

Sarah came to the table with the bacon. Her dark hair and gray eyes still attracted him. After two children, she had worked to keep her figure and was only a few pounds over her wedding weight.

Rudy had already selected his slices of toast. Rejecting tomatoes, he now chose his bacon carefully.

"Everything okay with the third grade?" Richard asked his wife.

"Fine."

They had both long remembered the day they met as undergraduates, when she had told him that her desire in life had been to teach children. When Richard had pressed her, she'd said the third grade would be the perfect age. He couldn't relate to that as a literature major, couldn't really see himself working with kids, but he did like the way she explained some pedagogy and sometimes tried to get him to extend or clarify his thinking. It had almost worked to keep him in school, until he'd finally given up on the desire for a career in literature.

She sat down and they began to make their sandwiches.

"You remember that you are taking Rudy with his youth group on Saturday," Sarah said.

Richard nodded. "Yes, of course. Disneyland?"

"No, Dad, I already told you ten times. The water park. Right?"

Richard asked, "Where's Manny?"

"In her room. I called her. Rudy, go get her."

"I will." Richard stood. "Can't miss her favorite meal."

He wondered suddenly, as he went to the hallway, what impression Emilia had formed of him. Though she seemed more and more familiar to him the longer he saw her—someone, a friend— he had to respect, after all, that she had a Ph.D. from out east. SUNY. She had a tenure track position at the Christian college near Pasadena. He had to respect that. And she was a grown woman, early thirties probably, though very young looking, perhaps because she was so small.

His own trajectory, if he could call it that, had happened fast. In his memory, he liked to think that it had been a gradual process, moving into what he had done with the rest of his life. The whole thing with following Sarah to the state school after community college and meeting the artistic, intellectual, skeptical Rachel, who was deciding to move to a better school for her, an art school on the East Coast. Their friendship had been intense and fun—she was leaving a relationship and seemed interested in him, but he had not acted fast enough to leave Sarah. Rachel, the first woman he had honestly loved, or at least been infatuated with, had gone east. They wrote a few times before he didn't return her last letter.

That was years ago. He had found Rachel finally on Facebook, just recently, but he hesitated to contact her. His own Facebook page had no pictures available to the unfriended, and his page listed his occupation merely as "In management."

Richard used his ring hand to open the door on his daughter's room. She was lying on her bed on her back.

"Don't you want a BLT?"

"They're making me sick," she said.

Richard thought he knew the signs. "Should I call a doctor." His voice did not rise at the end of his utterance. It was not a question.

"No. I just can't stand it. The smell is making me sick."

Richard stood for a moment. His real fear was an ulcer or a digestive track infection. But he asked, "You have a boyfriend I don't know about?"

"Dad, that's just cruel. I don't have a boyfriend. I just am sick of the smell of certain foods."

"Why?"

"Oh, because I'm sick of them." When Richard waited for more explanation, she rolled over and groaned.

Manny had been studying a popular book with her youth group that advocated not dating but something akin to the old style of courting. Richard wondered where in the Bible courting had been made explicit as a mating mechanism. Even in the Presbyterian Church Richard and Sarah had returned to after a five-year absence, there were these trends that started in the bookstores and breezed through the congregation. Certainly, where they were now, things were not as bad as at the non-denominational churches they had tried out. Richard was able to enjoy his occasional smoke. In Presbyterian circles this was guilt-free. But he bemoaned the fundies everywhere who marked reality spot-on in some chapter and verse arrangement. They were ever spot-on, with every answer 100 percent worth believing in, with no deviations, every word exact, every proper behavior spelled out before the end would come with the rise of the Anti-Christ in some country or political party not now in favor in the U.S.

And then he had heard the hopes of kids in Manny's youth group that one spouse would perfectly match them, that one fated lover waited in the wings for them in God's timing, even as they themselves were spot-on elect. The whole thing was troubling. Certainly they were better off trying to understand and help each other than to expect a perfect Ken to their Barbie.

Richard looked at his daughter and the paperback copy of *The Poisonwood Bible* from school opened on the floor. She'd barely started it. "Well then, I guess I'll get to eat your bacon tonight."

"Go ahead."

He continued to stare at her there on her bed. Lately there had been aberrations in her behavior, dishonesty. Bags of chips had disappeared, a bag of chocolates gone, with the wrapper turning up in her wastebasket when he emptied it last Saturday.

People had to keep up appearances.

Sarah tired easily during the week, and on the weekends she tended to fall asleep before 9 p.m. Richard's desire for her at the end of the week, when he came home after his Friday night shift, which was always the busiest night of the weekend, was always unabated. But lately she was asleep when he got home.

Tonight he tried to get home right after his shift, but then he had to talk to one of the truck drivers who pulled in late, and finally came in to a quiet house. The living room light looked like it had been left on in a window for travelers. Manny was out somewhere with youth group friends. Sarah and Rudy had both gone to bed.

Richard undressed and lay down next to a sleeping Sarah. Listening to her breathing, he thought about Emilia. She had been almost hurtful to him two days ago. And he had not heard from her about another meeting. Things seemed to be up in the air. What had changed in their discussion was uncertain to him, but her talking about changing her students' attitudes had the effect of putting him on notice. And her being late had seemed all of a piece with the rest of it.

The neighbor dog barked in the yard next door. Richard had met Emilia in another coffee shop where he went for a store managers' meeting in Pasadena. She was serving in the shop and very friendly when he told her he was "in management." Later, after a few meetings, she confessed that she only worked there weekends during the university semester. Richard only eventually learned or figured out the part about giving her a better footing with men. "Men don't want to talk to you," she had said, "if they learn too early that you have more education than they do." Then she had added, "So, what sort of management are you in, Ricky Martin?" She had liked calling him Ricky Martin after the old pop celebrity. He had seemed to be of real interest to her, and this was a new feeling. He hadn't had this sort of attention in a long time. And it was coming from someone as important as Emilia.

Richard had dropped out of college following his junior year after transferring from a community college. He had left school, he had told everyone, to write books, but he had then gone back to D&S to work and eventually, putting Sarah through her credentialing program, had become what he had become, first a dairy department manager and then store manager—with a constant paperback with his name on it in the break room. Marty had once encouraged him, saying something like, "That's just great, Rich. Shows you know people," or something like that. Literature had its uses. Even in the grocery business.

Richard rolled over and as he put his arm on Sarah's side, she started and then rolled away from him. He would have to hope to catch her first thing in the morning, except that he had to be in the store again first thing at 7:30 a.m. Long gone were the days when she'd get up to give him breakfast and see him off. And then after lunch he had to be available for Rudy's youth group.

The afternoon after work raged on into a tired raggedness at the water park where Richard sat watching the backpacks and the towels and purses. At midday, surely at a point of saturation, the other adults had checked their watches and thought of leaving after a few more rides. He'd seen them do it. Richard was already finished with the place. Resting next to an open bag of chips, he pulled on the side of his t-shirt that had begun to dry after he was splashed walking to their table. Now, he saw the bee land on his son's soft drink and work its way through the plastic lid. Richard allowed this. Rudy was done with it anyway.

He had long noted the similarities between this place and Disneyland rides, with the long, snaking lines which narrowed and corralled real desires into teen expectations of racy runs, all pushed to the edge but all too predictable, all suburban and boring. All led back to the same soft landing. Everyone screamed, laughed at being pushed to the edge of gravity and then brought back. No one would be sued; no one would be any wiser.

After about ten minutes, Richard watched the bee climb out of the cup and fly off. Then he picked up the cup, brought it to the trash, and then returned to the table and marked with his wallet where the cup had been. He stared off into the distance at the water rides and the kids screaming.

When two bees flew in and hovered around the original spot of Rudy's cup in a few minutes, it occurred to Richard that he had discovered that the hive must be close. Two more flew in behind them and they all hovered over his wallet. Richard again had only admiration for them, for their conciseness. Perhaps, he thought, dances were really better than words. He tried to consider this but found himself staring vaguely over the benches at the sun glistening in the blue pool water where a small girl came sliding into and making a splash.

Richard was on hand on Sunday morning to open the back door to the dairy truck when it arrived. As the truck lift lowered the first boxes and crates, Richard looked out at the retaining wall and smoked. The milk dollies dripped onto the pavement and cottage cheese crates smelled of the central cooler. It was always sunny out, he thought, and he listened to the chorus of birds.

The dairy truck driver went by, rolling a two-wheeler full of cheeses, and told him his name tag was slanted, but when Richard looked down he noticed that he had buttoned his vest wrong. This driver was playful in the way he drew attention to mistakes. He did it by giving the impression of the appearance, as though the mistake was the intention. That was his way when he went down the chip displays months ago and said something about the box under the display being too small. When Richard examined it, he saw that the cardboard display had been put together wrong. Richard had righted it. Now, as he unbuttoned his vest to make it right, he wondered where his name tag had disappeared to. It would be a week before the front office would replace this temporary one.

The morning was unusually slow, and Richard let Jason punch out and go home for an hour or two while he helped with the bagging. As he filled the plastic bags in the front and offered to take groceries to cars for the more elderly customers, he had a memory of a D&S store from decades ago that had included a customer pickup. At the front of the store was a sliding door where they wheeled the carts out with numbers and the hose across the lane in front would cause a bell to ding as in an old filling station when a car pulled up for a cart loading. Some customers would press their cart number, written on their receipt, against the car window. Others would have to get out and open their trunk with the ignition key. That was right on the cusp of the new technologies for trunk unlatching. Now, of course, there were parking spaces along the front of the store.

Richard found himself thinking about the world being replaced by computer technology. His kids were growing up today with computers and not books. They had spell check, of course, but the absence of hyperlinks in books to explain difficult words was increasingly making books alien to them.

Going to the backroom to sign for a produce truck, he saw his Richard Foster novel next to the coffee pot. It truly was odd that he did that. Most of the employees just sort of humored him. The only people he knew who still read, besides Emilia, of course, were the ladies at church.

The intercom sounded and Mickey was calling him to the front. Someone wanted to speak to him about an identification card.

He went forward, again in that funk where the people around him seemed to have no imagination when it came to other people, and the self-help industry that sometimes sponsored the seminars he was asked to attend had rendered reality slack, a large time-out between steps of efforts forward. Richard felt suddenly that they were really all doomed. Too many sunny days would need to be paid for, and they'd be sunk under the sea with nothing to mark them except a sign on a map pointing to what once had been Disneyland, a place now fabled and underwater. This was sure to be the end.

He was thinking of this end as he turned the paper and soap aisle and, before he reached Mickey's register, saw Emilia standing with her.

He thought to turn around, but in the moment he hesitated, she saw him and met his eyes. "I thought that you would need this," she said, and held up his name tag.

He came up to her. "So, how did you get this? And, there's no identification problem."

"Just this one," Emilia said and handed his name tag to him. "So this is what you mean by being 'in management.'"

Richard glanced off at the iPod display.

"You know," she said, "there were lots of Richard or Ricky Martins online, as you would expect. But it was your name tag that allowed me to pinpoint your profile and find you spot-on."

"I'm not profiled." His voice seemed to weaken.

"Everyone is. Look, Ricky, I'm Catholic. I don't believe in ruining marriages."

"I didn't expect you to," Richard said.

"Please don't call again. Life's short."

He realized that he was avoiding eye contact, and that he probably would not be able, years hence, to tell what she was wearing today, even as he had not remembered Rachel's style of dress the last times he saw her before her move to New York.

He wandered back through the frozen foods section, where he peered through the clear window at the case of frozen pizzas. You could take them out and enjoy hot pizza in minutes. He became aware that he stared into the case. Over the store intercom, the old Heart song played. "He's a magic man. . ." Ann Wilson moaned. "Try, try, try to understand. . .He's a magic man."

Where he stood, he realized that sustained thought would not be possible. The song stopped, and in the silence of the intercom, the store had a buzzing that he hadn't thought about for a long time.

Subtle Man Loses His Day Job

An Origin Story

This all happened after I quit college and before I started applying to Heinz and the GM plant in town. At the time, Winky wasn't even that much in the picture. He was this short, scrawny, slightly older guy, divorced I thought, and not of much interest, except he would say occasional surprising things that made people in Side Step laugh. His name—Winky—seemed like a cover. But other than that and his few jokes, he wasn't remarkable. He didn't stand out. When I think about it now, that's how I see it. I didn't hang around him. I didn't care to learn his real name, and I didn't notice when he started to become a central figure around Side Step until I was shooting pool there for about a month. And then he was still there. And it seemed normal that he'd head out to Denny's after closing Side Step with us. It seemed normal to think of him as part of us. Then I started to talk to him at some afternoon breakfasts, before heading down to the bar, and we had a lot in common. He found out that I'd tried to major in philosophy, and he was asking questions. Sometimes I'd try to bait him, play with his seriousness about whether life had a purpose. But I also started to be protective of the little guy, because after the long nights and early breakfasts, he was one of us. That's how I thought of him. He was one of us. Like all of us, nothing special, but special because he was one of us.

I doubt now that Winky was his name.

I doubt just about everything now.

After that first month, what I think really bonded us was that we started talking about the trip, which was my idea, over about seven cups of coffee one morning after closing Side Step. I told him about my hitchhiking exploits. At twenty-one, that's about all I had. Over the next few months, I regaled him with most of my true hitchhiking encounters. He started owning all of this, started talking about traveling and was convinced that we should go.

The truth is that I liked talking about the trip to California more than I liked going there. I liked talking about it because it was something to pass the time. I actually understood that without the trip coming up, there was nothing to talk about. It seemed like we were already on our own journey. He added to things I was saying, and suddenly he was like an evangelist. Everybody in Side Step was talking about it. Phil gave me his questioning look. Then Winky got Liz interested in going with us. This is when it became real, because with Liz, we suddenly had a car and a way to travel. He had this persuasion about him, especially when it came to a cause. For example, when he found out I was trying to get into the local factories, he tried to convince me to go for something better. He convinced me that I was selling myself short. He believed that I should keep up with philosophy.

The trip had become this symbol of how our lives were going to improve and become more fulfilled, if we would just get out of town. And Liz was coming with us, and her car was going to be our transportation. When push came to shove, though, I realized I didn't want to go to California again. Winky kept up with it, seemed ready to leave at a moment's notice. He was completely in. He was saving his money. I didn't save anything, not even on my last paycheck waiting tables. That last night in town, I started boozing it up extra heavy, even buying rounds, and it went unnoticed. If Winky is who I now think he claims he is, then I'm surprised he didn't notice. I wasn't subtle about it at all. I realized something. I preferred being right here, with friends in Side Step.

I waited to tell him about all of this, about my lack of funds. We left, moving north, and after a day we were just about out of the Upper Peninsula, in a restaurant where Winky was counting his money, had it all laid out there on the table. Liz had just gone to the bathroom.

We looked like bank robbers, with Winky our gang leader spreading all that cash out. I chuckled and looked around, but the tables near us were empty. Then I sulked. It wasn't the money that brought me down and made me say it. He was going on about the newspaper as he looked over his money. He was like that. Always counting his stuff. Always folding his socks and laying them out to make sure he had enough for the week.

"Somebody clearly benefits from melodrama in the news," he said.

"Who reads newspapers anymore?" I looked at him seriously.

"Somebody clearly benefits," he repeated.

Clearly? How was it clear? I blinked, my way of letting on that I begged to differ. I was younger than he was, but I felt older, more experienced. I was bigger. I had solved a few barroom fights with my fists. He was abstract, living in his head.

"Dualistic," he said. This was a word he used often. Sometimes, I would push him there just for the fun of it. I'd set it all up, he'd have too much to drink, and then I'd wait for him to go there.

"Good and evil," he harangued. "Current events are a corollary to the movie industry. As though we are watching a movie of our lives, and we can send in the usual action figures to just 'clean up.' It's the American, dualistic, 'damn the torpedoes' Way." Then he seemed really put out about it. He hadn't seen me blinking and frowning, even though I was making it super obvious. I know what our mutual friend Phil would have said. If this were going on back in the Side Step Tavern, which I was missing already, Phil would have countered with the fact that the Thirties led to comic books, and people were then able to survive through the worst of the depression and then war. And that's what the movies did for us, then as now. Then we would have had a great debate over comics and then some pool games. But that night, out there on the Wisconsin border, without Phil there, all I remember was thinking, man, I've got more of this to look forward to for how long?

"There is no room in this world for something, say, more. . .between the lines." He looked at me and his sincerity made me want to laugh. I don't mean a good-natured laugh. I mean derisive. I wanted to laugh at him.

"You know what I mean?" He looked at me. "Something that doesn't fit our normal categories."

I smiled. "You mean, like having four limbs, two eyes, and a nose?"

"Yes, exactly. But not quite."

I didn't know that this was a friendship at its turning point. I shrugged. "I only have twenty-six dollars."

Winky looked like he hadn't heard me. He finally asked, "You mean you only have twenty-six dollars?"

I nodded.

"You mean that literally," he said. "Not symbolically."

"I can buy our dinner. Or I can buy smokes in the morning, coffee once. And then I'm broke. Literally."

Liz returned, sat down. She was in a blue tank top and folded her arms. "We leaving?"

"Neal only has twenty-six dollars."

"Oh," Liz said. "I knew that."

Winky started to pick up his money. "What do we do now? I can't turn around."

I didn't understand why he couldn't turn around. I realize that he was in his early thirties or late twenties or something, and he'd been divorced and saw this as a fresh start. But those six months when I was talking up the trip, I realized that I loved where I was. Didn't Winky also? I had my friends in Side Step. Liz had been a part of that scene, too, and I was surprised to see my talk inflating her hopes. As for Winky, I thought that he could have just gone back with me. What else should a guy like him do? What was on the west coast? Jobs? I'd been there two years ago. But you don't know how the Winkys of the world will build their little castles in the air. I can't be blamed for that. Plenty of drunks talk big, but nothing ever comes of it except a trip to the john.

Who named him Winky, anyway?

We continued on the northern route I'd mapped out, through Minnesota and North Dakota. We went as far as Seattle, camped, woke up in the rain, and then drove to the city for coffee and looked for work. My lack of funds had led Winky to cast this as plan B. We looked for work in Washington. We spent two weeks. I shared a tent with Liz. I don't know if Winky could hear us from his tent at night, but I stopped caring. I had weed. He probably smelled it. I would have shared it, but he'd stopped really talking much, and it was best to have someone not cross-eyed out there. The one evening I did offer him weed, he wasn't in his tent. I found him standing in a place on the campgrounds looking over the river that ran below along the highway. It was a place where he could see past the trees to the horizon. He stood there a long time without noticing me. I know it sounds clichéd, but I thought I saw him reach out and try to grab something from the sky. Maybe I didn't. It was weird and I was high, and maybe it was my high school reading coming back to haunt me.

Anyway, after I told Liz about it that night and we laughed about it, I forgot about that until later.

After two weeks, we had a meeting. Winky could pay for our bus fare back home. Liz could keep going in her car and make it to her sister's in a few days.

I remember the silence as Liz drove us to the Seattle Greyhound.

The night we returned in July, with Winky behind me, I took a breath, yanked open the door, and walked into the familiar de-compress of cigarettes, booze, video game lights, and the greasy tacos of the Side Step Tavern.

"Dean," I shouted at the first familiar face I saw.

"What?" He seemed annoyed. The resident communist, he stood up from the bar with difficulty due to some nonspecific disability in his legs or back. Because he complained of problems with both, Mike, the owner, allowed him to bring his Doberman in.

At a table near the door, Phil nursed a draft and fingered his voice recorder—what he used for his "research." A few regulars sat with him. He stared at me for a long moment.

"So," he said, "you came back after all."

I sat down. Next to me, Winky stiffened as Dean moved over to our table and his dog sniffed him.

"Trotsky," Dean said. Then he eyed Winky. "So you don't like dogs."

"Not Dobermans," Winky said.

"I didn't notice this before." Dean narrowed his eyes. "Is it just Dobermans? Usually my dogs like people. How would you feel if I brought in Khrushchev?" Khrushchev was his German shepherd.

I held out my hands. "What kind of a welcome is this?"

"Yeah. So you're back." Dean eyed Winky. I hadn't noticed animosity between them before. "So, where'd you go?"

"Seattle."

"Oh. I was going to say Oregon. Close, anyway." Dean picked up part of a taco in front of him and tossed it to his dog.

"I could see you coming back," Phil said to me. Then he looked up at Winky. "But what's your take on it?"

"He's getting his old job back," I said. "It's all good."

"All good, huh?" He shook his head, as though he'd expected as much all along. "Okay, boys," and then he pushed his voice recorder aside.

"What's this?" I asked him.

He picked up his deck of cards. "This?" He seemed to like the attention. "This is something I'm saving for later. I think that if you have read DC or Marvel, you should hear it."

Phil shuffled the deck. "It may be that this adds a complication and deepening to things." He split the deck. "For now, though, we have four hands. So how about some Euchre?"

"Think I'm going to go," Winky said.

"How does it deepen things?" I asked.

Phil dealt two handed. And without Winky for the first time in a month, back at Side Step, this was life.

I won. Then I shot pool. And the crowds ebbed and flowed around Side Step. At one point a party of people in tuxedos and formal dress came through.

When I was about to shoot another game of pool, Phil motioned to me to sit down with the others who'd sat at his table, and he turned on his recorder and hit pause.

"DC, Marvel, you know have heroes with powers they came upon through exposure to radioactivity. Some came from other planets."

"Radiation. They knew so much in the fifties," Dean said.

"But now, what if there's another way of looking at it? What if we have human potential that lies within us, and we have not yet learned to tap into it?"

The quiet deepened around the table. Someone laughed two tables away, and the sound of billiard balls clacking together came through.

"So what, are we talking human potential movement on steroids?" Dean said.

"Or something lost in the fall," Phil said.

"You mean before winter comes?" Pete asked.

"He means the fall from grace. The fruit of the tree of good and evil." Dean rubbed under his dog's neck.

"Well if that were the case, wouldn't people be flying out of churches and saving the world?"

"Exactly," Phil said. "What if this is the next stage? I just ask, 'What if?'"

What kept me there in that moment was not the idea, but what was unique, at least in my experience, to Side Step: The familiar mix of untrained philosophy and alcohol. I was glad to be back. So as Phil took the pause off his recorder and his voice came through, I sat back.

"So what about the other?" Phil could be heard saying on his voice recorder. "Not the day job, but the other."

"What about it?" said another voice.

"When did it start? How did it start? And. . .anything else you could tell."

"Well, the first time I saw myself as a hero, I mean, as myself, it had to do with my day job. I had quit college and took a job working for the state. I was doing file stuff in a workers' compensation firm that our former Democratic governor had decided to buy to help with funding to make the state more business friendly. I was filing and helping with cases by day. It was a great day job. At night, I was checking out the people filing the cases. Yes, it felt awkward. Some people take years to recognize themselves. And they take even longer to accept it. But I recognized that I was being subtle, and I found that I was saving the firm money when it was also losing money. I was researching the cases I was getting and finding more fraud than I thought possible. I was doing this without being noticed. I was Subtle Man.

"And then, just when my movement at night began to really branch out, moving from fraud cases to some things going on within the firm, I lost my day job. The firm went belly-up. After just six months as a state firm, it went bankrupt. I was let go, even though my cases were actually saving the firm money.

"And of course I was young and married, and I had to act fast, and I had no degree. I took a night job in a care facility for the elderly. I thank the gentle, aged patients in the home who accepted me. Granted, most of them were probably not processing that a man in tights was sitting with them, listening to their impossible dreams of having their families and their old lives come back to them."

In the recording, Phil said, "I think that everyone will want to know what incident brought you out?"

"I know. You are looking for a lost alien ship or a school bus sinking into the river with fifty kids about to drown. But I'm different. I'm Subtle Man."

"No, I'm not talking about that."

"Everyone does. I mean subconsciously. But that's not my angle. The first incident—I solved a Medicare scam at the home.

It was easy. I noticed unlocked drug cabinets that would stay unlocked until just before dawn. And the med counts were off, especially Mr. Sampler's morphine for his recent surgery to remove one lung. So I took the lock that was hanging there undone, photocopied the nightly schedule, circled the names, and brought this into my supervisor's office and put it in her desk drawer. I also placed a card on which I'd drawn my logo—a blue and gray emblem that resolved itself—if you paid attention to it—into an S. I admit I used to play with that at home before my wife got back from teaching.

"The next day, Pat Hand, the supervising nurse, ordered drug tests. The nurse and the other night janitor quit.

"Pat Hand pinned my card to the employee bulletin board. It stayed there a long time, generated conversation."

"And you never had any doubts about yourself?"

"Doubts?"

"Oh, say, that you were deluded?"

"No. I never doubted."

At our table, with the music on in the back ground, Pete said, "First warning flag."

"First?" said Nick, who sat with an empty shot class.

"To you listening, whoever you are going to be," the recorded voice said, "this is not a mythical account. I don't have the typical 'origin story' you seek. I represent the human heart, those first steps into the taboo and the underworld. Because when you do that, you discover that America is, largely, a great underworld. You don't just plan to be a superhero. Look at the hero archetypes of Campbell and Jung. For me, it was as though with each step I took, more light dawned. It was slow, as though I could see my very hands transforming before my eyes."

When he got to the part about America and Campbell and Jung, I recognized something. I didn't think it possible. I miss a great many things because I don't think they are possible. But the thought did come that this was Winky. I dismissed it. Winky was too shy. If I hadn't been the one to push going out to California, he would still have been stuck back in the kitchen at Gino's Pizza. Well, actually, now that I thought about it, he still was stuck there.

"But you want the heroic stuff," the voice said. "What I have is a failure, the fateful night when the new janitor went down to the next wing to mop the floor. I stepped into my secret room—the janitor's closet—and stripped to my uniform. And in that moment, slender arms embraced me, and I heard Pat Hand's voice. 'Marvel Comics? Sexy.' And she turned me around and began to kiss me.

"I'd turned her on.

"'Mmm,' she said. 'I got your card. I'm not that dumb.' She laughed. 'So many nights and you must not see your wife.'

"'Pat, I need to apologize, I—'

"'I get it. You're Catman,' she said. 'You are so quiet, so, so subtle. No one knows. Like a cat.' I hadn't thought of that connection, I'll admit. As she ran her hand down my chest, past my emblem of a blue and gray overlapping of shapes that when looked at finally resolves into an S, I thought momentarily that 'Catman' would be a better hero than Subtle Man. And then I became distracted because I saw her, not as my boss, but as a sexual being, as a woman.

"'Don't you think others have lost the power to see?' I asked.

"'Shh.' Her finger was over my lips. 'Don't talk.'

"'Superman may have powers that we've lost, perhaps, but everyone has certain powers.'

"'Don't talk.' She breathed heavily. 'No one needs to know.' She unbuttoned her blouse.

"'How long have you suspected?'

"'A while.' And she licked my upper lip.

"'This costume isn't a sex thing. It's real.'

"'It sure is.'

"Then my blunder. I'm sure that telling this will cast doubt on my subtlety. I said, 'I'm happily married.'

"I watched it dawning on her. 'It's real? You mean, it's, the costume, is real?'

"'My marriage? Of course.'

"'No.' She stepped back and looked me up and down. 'This. This is real.'

"The next day I was told not to report to work. I tried to talk to Pat. When I did get her on the phone, she said, very softly, 'If it was just sex, that would be one thing. Happens all the time in this very dull job. But you really believe you can leap from tall buildings—'

"'I never said that. I am gifted with subtlety.'

"But I had been exposed. My marriage ended. I had to leave."

Dean pet his dog Trotsky. "Hahaha, ohmyGad, a fruitcake."

"Has a kind of poetry to it," Phil said. "This guy reads books."

"So he passes your first rule for a superhero worthy of attention," I said. "Intelligence. Well, sort of. Who is he?"

"He was wearing a ski mask," Phil said. "I don't know. What's it sound like he looks like? What do you think? Buff? Seven feet? Or does size even matter? When a super acts, that's when he or she is larger than life."

"So he looks like a wimp," said Pete.

"He's got biceps and powerful legs, strength in subtle places for sudden bursts of energy." Phil looked at Dean.

"That's no superhero," Dean said. "That's just your average, over-compensating psycho who's stopped taking his meds."

Phil said, "Healthy skepticism is called for here, of course."

"Some people need an outlet," Dean said. "You got comic books. He needs a hobby. Photography, say."

"Photography?"

"Yeah, photography."

Phil laughed.

"Okay," Dean said, "What's he done?"

"He stopped a Medicare rip-off."

"I coulda done that." Dean stood up, leaned on his cane.

Pete, who worked in a meat department and was trying to get promoted and usually came in wearing a tie, said, "If he's a super, what are his powers? Okay, he's intelligent. But what are his powers? What can he do?"

"I'm thinking this is something more like maybe someone out of the Watchmen. I'm still cataloguing this," Phil said. "This is a real encounter. I didn't make this up to fit a theory."

"Intelligence," Dean said. "Listen to you losers." He limped for the door.

I asked Phil, "Is this someone we know?"

He looked at me and then turned away. "I can't say. But the whole superhero thing, lulls of incompetent normalcy, followed by archetypal heights. It's all here."

In that moment I realized how much I had missed Phil.

Later, at Phil's, we found our candidate at "NewAmerican-Heroes.com." There was the usual run of cops, firemen, and service men. There was a doctor. And then there was Subtle Man. His strengths were listed: "intelligence, speed, an ability to haunt dreams." Then we went over to Wikipedia, where Subtle Man's kind of intelligence was given a special definition, explained as intuition. Subtle Man relied on something "once attributed to the angels of the middle ages," the website claimed. He had lightning intuition. He apprehended wholes faster than normal minds. One commentator questioned his origin: Was Subtle Man in fact an angel?

This was what we found on Wikipedia.

The trouble with this superhero, also noted, had to do with dogs. A mythical struggle engaged him between heaven—his intuition—and hell—going to the dogs.

Over the next few weeks, I got back into things. One morning, I ate breakfast and relaxed, I realized, without Winky. We'd come back and gotten a room together, but we were on different schedules. I loved the town, where I'd gone to school for a while, a small college town that also had factories.

As I sat in my window seat looking out on the main strip, Winky passed by and then came in and sat down as he had so many times before our trip. "I can't stay," he said. "I have to work."

The waitress brought him coffee and he refused it. "My plan is to get back out west by October."

"Really?"

"Monica has a car. You and I influenced a lot of people before we left. A lot of people. Monica was interested, and I didn't even know it. I was working with her, and I didn't even see it. Monica and I, we can go in two months."

"Another rape last night," I said, unfolding the newspaper. I studied him. "More news melodrama?"

"The rape was like the others," Winky said.

"Huh?"

"New girl in town, staying out by the Lakeside. Cops should be checking for strange cars in the area, for someone hiding out there, or profiling the residents."

I stopped chewing. "I learned about a new hero last night. I understand this Subtle Man has the intuition of angels."

"Who's Subtle Man?"

"You left, though, before you could hear about him. Whaddaya know about nursing homes?"

"I hope to avoid putting my parents in one. I know there are good ones. But even with Dad's properties, we can't afford those."

So he was still set on moving. I felt guilty. I had planted this in his strange head. I'd built it up, this dream I had realized was just nostalgia, a dream long over.

That night, I went to Gino's, saw Monica in a sleeveless, flowery blouse. I had never seen her wear anything low-cut. Her hair was wavy, and her blue eyes were not seductive; they were delft eyes, large, childish flowers reflected in bloom.

And now she and Winky were going out west. She was probably ripe—that's how I thought of her—and Winky was just "other worldly" enough to not push the physical. Suddenly, I envied them.

"Can I help you?" she asked, and then looked up from folding a pizza box. "Oh," she said. "He's not here. He left an hour ago with some friends."

"Friends?" I said. Winky had friends? I mean, besides me?

I wandered back to Side Step. It was a slow night. I nursed a very weak light beer on tap. I usually tried one of the craft beers that Mike would put on tap. This wasn't a craft night, though.

After I left, I passed an all-night café and saw Winky sitting with four Mexicans.

At our apartment, I read until midnight, when there was loud knocking.

It was Phil. "Oh boy," he said. "You're not going to believe this."

In Denny's, Phil stirred milk into his coffee. "Just can't believe it. I thought he was something else. But he's dark, definitely dark. This is a twist."

"Who?"

"Subtle Man."

"Just your average psychopath finding his way in today's world," I said.

Phil set his spoon down on a napkin. "If I had a constant way of recording, I'd enter it in the record. Subtle Man is dark. My cousin has a desk job in the police department. I've been talking to him. He told me tonight that a guy in a ski mask and tights helped the rapist to get away."

"You seem more concerned with how your comic book will play out than you do about stopping a rapist."

He was brooding.

"You know who this is," I said. "You actually talked to him. You have no superhero law of silence to obey. You need to turn him in. Your superhero got in the way of solving this. This is the way the comics happen in real life."

Crows' feet deepened around his eyes. "Maybe."

"You're the man with the recordings. You can help. No, you need to."

"I only saw him in his ski mask. I couldn't tell you who he is."

"You need to tell them everything." I glanced back at the couple coming in the front doors and standing at the waiting area for the hostess.

"This is sad. I just keep looking for another way." He stared at his coffee. "Something's going on here, and you're concerned with outing a friend."

"Friend?" I said.

"Yes, friend. I mean someone I've started to think of as our friend." He leaned forward. "If Subtle Man helped the rapist escape, is there another explanation? I'd like to know, and that's all I'm saying. It's not about some damned comic book farce to me. This is real."

"Damned right it's real. Real as the Unabomber." That was over the top, but so was this conversation.

The next night, the front door to Side Step swung open and Dean stood there with both dogs. Two drunks shrieked and the Doberman yanked at the chain and pulled Dean forward onto his bad leg and attacked a kid sitting with his dad at a table near the video games.

Dean had also read the Wikipedia account of Subtle Man, and he pulled his dogs back and the door to the tavern opened again.

"I'll find him," Dean said. "Trotsky and Khrushchev got a huge scent tonight. Nothing truer than a dog's nose."

I looked at the strange dot on Khrushchev's nose.

I went home early that night. He wasn't there, so I went for proof. I went in and trashed Winky's room. I pulled all his clothes from his closet, all his notes, looking for evidence of his former employment with a nursing home. But true to the friend I had known, Winky was not nostalgic. He had no evidence of anything before his living here. Finally, I took one of his t-shirts from his laundry basket.

I didn't see Winky all that morning or afternoon, and that evening when I stopped at Gino's, he told me he'd stayed the night with Monica.

"Who are your new friends?" I asked him.

"What new friends?"

"Monica said you were out with some new people."

"Oh, just a couple of workers up from Texas. They are looking for work and starting at the shop and had some questions about one of Dad's rental properties."

I shook my head. He went back to the kitchen, and I went across the street. I had to wait a long time that night for anyone to show up. I shot pool and drank Jack Daniels. I also noticed the appearance of a well-dressed Mexican dude. He had been at the bar two nights a week now checking things out. He looked to be from some Mediterranean port or somewhere from a wealthy province in Mexico. He spoke good English. Maybe he was an American.

By the time Dean showed up that night with his dogs, I was slurring my speech.

Just as I had held Winky's t-shirt in front of Trotsky and Khrushchev, gave them both a great whiff of it, Winky came in and said in his voice that hurt with injustice, "My room was trashed. Somebody broke in."

The dogs lunged after him and he ran, scared, back to Gino's. I thought that was enough proof.

Later that night, I came home and found Winky was packing his stuff. He was moving in with Monica for a few nights. So I confessed the whole thing, including my suspicions. This made his mind up finally. He moved everything out that night. At the end of it, I slept soundly in the quiet, and I only noticed the next morning that I still had the t-shirt I had taken from him.

As the sun went down at the end of Main Street, the well-dressed man from the Mediterranean came in and sat across the bar with a glass of wine. He sat next to Tanker, from whom I usually got my stash. I hadn't needed to talk to him since I'd gotten back, and looking at this arrangement, I decided I was lucky not to. I walked out on the pavement, and as I moved down the street to buy more smokes, I could smell the approach of rain and a distant rumble of thunder. I thought about how to approach Tanker and his new connection. This would be just to find out. Apparently the man from the Mediterranean also wanted to score some. Across the street, under the street lights, Monica pulled out of Gino's lot in her Civic. She really had a fine figure. Winky was quite the man to have recognized this. Then I was depressed again. I wanted them both to stay. I was jealous for the old days.

Back in Side Step, the Mediterranean checked his watch. Tanker seemed nervous. What happened next was this: As I knocked my new smokes on the bar top, the front door opened, and the place was shaken by lightning—as though lightning had just struck the street right outside. The bar went dark, and then the lights went on, and I saw Subtle Man in the doorway. There was a cry and then Trotsky yelped in fear.

Subtle Man stared over the pool tables and shouted at the Mediterranean, "Rainbow Alley." Then he was gone.

There was a mad rush for the door. Dean fell and his dogs tore away and the man from the Mediterranean, with a pistol out, suddenly dragged Tanker, who was actually handcuffed to him, out the door.

I dropped back, kept my distance. When I slipped out into the rain now coming down, I was behind Phil and Dean, who had gotten up rubbing his shoulder after his dogs pulled him down. At Rainbow Alley, I was drenched as the police cruisers pulled in, their wipers splashing and their blue and red lights flashing against the dark windows of the buildings—an old sewing shop that was empty and a computer store. I heard the gun shots and Dean's dogs attacking someone, and then I saw Trotsky and Khrushchev tearing into someone, while his companion slipped and fell to his knees in the wet and was then pressed up against the wall and holding up his automatic weapon in surrender. Even in the rain, I thought I recognized the t-shirt he wore as one of Winky's. Khrushchev was snarling at him and two cops had their pistols aimed at his forehead.

Suddenly Dean shouted and pointed down the alleyway, where Subtle Man stood under the only building light. This distraction caused one of the cops to turn, and the suspect against the wall lowered his automatic weapon to shoot, and then was shot by the other cop who hadn't budged.

Subtle Man ran down the street to a car, and as it pulled away, I thought it was Monica's car I saw partially lit by the street light.

In the rain, I noticed all the cell phones out catching the moment.

Denny's that night buzzed with the accounts. Subtle Man was a drug dealer, an agent of the cartels. He was a rapist. He wanted chaos. Phil's cousin who worked for the police came in. The perps in the alley, he said, were from a cartel. They were trying to work their way in. And Tanker was the rapist. Subtle Man saw the connection and stopped the cops from arresting him before he could lead them to the cartel.

"Okay, Phil," I asked. "What will you do with your recordings?"

"Cops have them."

"You should tell this."

"He's headed for Hollywood."

I thought about it.

Phil eyed me. "Imagine. A Subtle Man in Hollywood."

I didn't laugh. "Disappointing. Subtle Man should champion complexities. Education. Psychology. Stopping a cartel in this little Michigan town is a sellout. I think he was driven by doubt. Had to prove himself, go big time."

Phil said, "Ah, Neal, you're just mad that he caught your source."

I shrugged. "He is a narc."

"There is always the human, unpredictable part. No one acts the perfect equation."

Phil never told me Subtle Man's identity, but he didn't have to. For me, the t-shirt gave it away. It was his way of communicating with me one last time. To this day, I can't remember if he ever smoked pot with us. I thought maybe he did once or twice at the beginning, just to fit in, just to seem like he was one of us. But maybe that's just something he led me to believe.

I looked for Winky's name in various California cities. I never found it or Monica's.

When the Heart Plays Dead

A s Carl Harding drove his family to the children's museum
downtown after lunch, they went by his old high school and
then the old music store, and he was reminded of his dream of
Deborah that morning just before he woke up. Deborah was the
girl he dated seriously in high school, and the music store, still
open, reminded him of the dream because Deborah had often
gone there to buy eight track tapes when they were together. He
had lost track of the people he had known when he lived here, and
now, when he came back with his family, the buildings, parks, and
streets stirred his memory. Places as topics. It was the old Greek
idea. Locations suggested things. For anyone else, the location
would tell a different story.

Carl thought it was because he was home again that he'd
dreamed of Deborah in a house full of shadow and sunlight that
vaguely resembled her house on Fulcrum Street, where she had
been waiting for him, and where Carl had somehow wandered
from his life, feeling a deep obligation to her. So much had passed
in the dream, so much of his life he'd not shared with her, and even
knowing this, he told her that they should marry. Next, he found
he was on a sidewalk with her and one of her friends. But before he
could reassert his proposal, the dream faded.

Carl missed the dream's importance. Dreams were like man-
holes to the everlasting. Even this dream had to be. It wasn't some
unmasking of his true desire. He could hardly know that.

The tickets to the children's museum weren't cheap, even with the coupons Carl's mother gave them. As soon as they paid, Elise, the older girl, drawn to the gumball machine, ran away, and Rebecca, younger by a year and a half, followed after. These places were not named right, Carl thought. They had sprung up all over the country, and Carl and Penny had been in several of them, in LA, in Indianapolis, in New Orleans, and they really weren't museums—places where there were artifacts on display. They were places where children could explore and play and discover things about a world carefully planned around them.

Carl turned to Penny, and he thought about why she had married him. It had been for true love, she insisted. He was beginning to think now, as their time together had begun to pull layers from them, that she had married him because he resembled her father, retired now, but once a high school teacher who wrote a weekly history column for his local paper. He wasn't sure why she saw her father in him. Perhaps he'd been too compliant, too much of a blank screen, and she was able to project her desires on him. Perhaps it was only because he was in books so much. When they visited her parents, Penny's father would work his latest explanations for some old building near the river into his conversations. He seemed to find great solace from these monologues, which started with buildings but ended with people and the ways in which the past could still be found in the present. Carl, of course, heard only conjunctions.

Penny showed no tolerance for it. She always left the room. When Carl told her about his old neighborhood when they were here, she would say "Put it on paper." This was not an encouragement to write so much as an invitation to stop talking.

Looking out the museum window at the park, he was puzzled that she would marry someone who had qualities she found to be annoying in a parent.

She came up beside him. "Rebecca is already in the light room. One of us should be there."

He glanced at her. "The place isn't very busy."

"Still."

He took her hand. "There's so much of the past still here."

"Well, yes."

"I see why people write memoirs. Of course it helps if they're famous."

"You should write a romance."

"But the only romance I've ever known ended tragically."

"Great first line," she said. "But alter it. Say 'The only *other* romance I ever knew ended tragically,' and then have your book end happily. After all, it did, didn't it?"

"Of course."

"Of course," she echoed.

He eyed her. Was she doubting him?

"You're just not a romantic," she said, letting go of his hand and picking up a blue-stoned bracelet for sale.

He viewed the bracelet between her fingers. "It's different for men. And anyway, yes I am a romantic."

"No you're not."

"No. I may not 'get romantic.' But I definitely am a romantic."

"Always the philosopher."

She left the trinkets and went to the next room where there were various experiments and tricks with light beams. Carl started to follow. Once, he had tried to tell Penny about Deborah. Just before the end of his junior year of high school, Deborah, a graduating senior, had sat with him in his basement and told her heartbreaking story of her relationship with an older man, who had dropped out of college and moved to California. Carl nodded and supported her like a good listener. She marveled at this and praised him for it, though as he thought about it, she was praising him for being timid, for it was really his way of not having to admit that he had never been in a relationship with a girl. And there was something emotionally appealing about Deborah. She wasn't exactly his type. But he'd not met anyone so tragic before, someone who had seen so much. On that Friday night in late spring, when she told her tragic story of Bruce, Carl found himself drawn to the edges of an inviting whirlwind.

For weeks after that, Carl lost his old fixations on the anatomy of some of the girls in his class. He felt for someone, his world changed by this girl who had left the scent of her perfume on the sofa in the basement where he did his homework every day.

When he later showed Penny what Deb had written in his junior yearbook, she said, "You fell for that?"

So he hadn't told her more about it.

But he also remembered why he had loved her. Pity had awakened a longing in him. This much Carl knew about himself: He was incapable of loving unless he pitied first.

That fall, his senior year, she started at the community college, and she told him she was not going to the Homecoming dance with him. Then she stopped calling at work.

Four months later, she joined the Army.

Carl began reading Hemingway after she was gone. He spent his senior year absorbing understatement and omitted details in narratives about broken young men. Secretly he hoped when the phone rang that it would be her again. After seven months, when spring came around again, he found that he could no longer stand the fluff he'd come to associate with her. To him, it was now emotional pornography. This understanding of her need for "language" drove him to avoid emotion. After high school he randomly decided to move to Chicago, where he took up boxing until he received a mild concussion, and then the gloves hung on the nail in the door of his closet in his one room apartment. He became accustomed to basic English in the commerce around him, reading signs like "Employees must wash their hands before returning to their work station" and "Caution: Bridge may be slippery" over and over again as though it were a kind of text, until he thought of language only in terms of basic instructions. It was at a point before the first snow fall that year in the city that he encountered his first human contact outside of the place where he was washing dishes when two young women wearing backpacks he talked to turned out later to be Moonies.

The following summer he moved home again to start college. Deborah's imagination he now saw as flimsily propped up on expectations borrowed from romance novels. He had hoped that in getting away from that and seeing someone new, he could revise the past and perhaps even discover what love really was about. Instead, he had met Moonies and an old lady who ran the cash register and chain smoked in the Italian restaurant where he'd worked.

Much later, in grad school he had joked with peers about how Hemingway had been his gateway author. Carl did wonder if his year of transience in Chicago before starting college hadn't done something to him, that it wasn't still the emotional tenor of his life now. He couldn't be sure.

Penny knew he'd gone to Chicago for a while, and they'd talked about a few places they both knew there. But that was it. He had never told her that he was able only to respond with pity, and he hadn't pitied anyone in a long time. This was the epiphany he'd been living with. With Penny, he had come to understand that his kindness and, after their wedding and first year together, his "being there" through the first of two pregnancies would help them settle into being happy together.

When they returned from downtown late in the day, the kids had fallen asleep in the car. Elaine, Carl's mother, stood at the door watching the sleeping kids as Carl and Penny each carried one inside and laid them on the bed in Carl's old room, which his mother had now set up as the guest room. Carl held Penny's hand and stroked her shoulder, but she lay down near the kids and mouthed, "I'm going to nap."

He said, "I have to tell you something."

She closed her eyes. "Can it wait?"

He glanced at her chin and then the way that her hands were folded on her stomach. Next to her, the girls drew on sleep like deep sea divers on oxygen. "I suppose."

She opened her eyes. "What is it?"

"It can wait."

"You sure?"

"I only feel pity."

"For who?"

"For whom. For everyone."

"That's good."

"The only way I can love is by looking down."

"I don't understand."

There was a dank odor in the weaving of the bedspread. "I want—" He glanced up at Elise, who slept profoundly. "I want you to know that I want to love you. I mean, I've tried to be romantic."

"Well, keep trying."

It was the assurance that came with the wedding for her, that he was always, till death, going to be here. He—they—could keep trying. "I don't know why I've never been able—" He stopped himself.

"Yeah?"

"To understand this about myself."

Her eyes were closed.

He pursed his lips. "Do you think. . ."

"Yes, I think."

"Is love even possible?"

"With two kids? I would hope so."

"I see."

"You see what?"

"Nothing," he said.

The picture of his sister's wedding in the center of the wall had dust on the frame. Carl turned to the window.

"Well, I'd like to sleep," she said.

"I just don't know what I'm trying to tell you."

"I'm going to sleep," she said.

He stood and the bed lifted up.

He wanted her to take his account of this and give it her better perspective. He watched her breathing as it raised her chest up and down and her heartbeat gently continued.

On the patio in the back yard, under the budding trees, Carl sat on the lawn chair. He opened his notebook to a blank page and thought of the old places here in town renewed by commercial designs. Of course, his life was elsewhere now. Life had moved on.

Carl wrote on the first line on the blank page of his notebook. "What romance I knew ended tragically." We need the language, he thought, to lead us in, to make it real. What there seemed to be were only the glances, the signs of the rushing pulse, the elements of desire that later, in marriage, would be taken for lust. What was needed—words—seemed not to come. At least about words, Deborah had been on the right track after all.

He thought about where to take Penny tonight. The first thought was a movie, but there were none they wanted to see.

The wind came up through the trees. Just down the hill, where he had once played with a whole neighborhood full of kids, the trees had grown in.

The budding branches waved above him, and then the door to the breezeway screeched open. His older daughter walked out. She rubbed her face and yawned. She sat down quietly, composed, in the lawn chair next to him, looked out for squirrels, Carl thought, or maybe a rabbit.

She folded her hands, like Carl's, though she didn't have a notebook. She yawned again.

"How did you sleep, beautiful?" he asked her.

"Fine." She smacked her lips.

Carl nodded.

"Did you grow up here?" she asked him suddenly.

"Yes." And then, as though trying to pick out the exact place where the world was larger and there was more time, and his small child's place in it seemed vital every moment, Carl lifted his arm and pointed into the trees. "I used to play here with all the other kids in the neighborhood."

She squinted hard momentarily, trying really to see something there, kids from the past doing things she might know, but then looked down at her fingers, which moved repetitiously forming figures in her lap.

"I don't like hot sauce," she said.

"I know you don't."

"That's what grown-ups like."

"Yep."

"When I'm grown up, I will like it."

"You sure?" he asked her. "You don't have to. Many people don't."

"I don't like hot sauce now. But when I grow up I will."

Carl nodded. "We'll see about that."

Man in the Army Jacket without Medals

L ater, I heard it said of a hundred towns across the Midwest what I first heard said of my hometown. A bar and a church could be found on every corner. And while not literally true, the stereotype did capture something about the options local people felt for themselves. Between the neon signs for beer and hard liquor and the corner marquees with upbeat quotes posted by local pastors, the two industries doted the marketplace with competing views of human possibility. Though the two segments of humanity in my hometown seemed to be aware of the other living nearby, sort of in the way cousins recognize each other, a line hardened by habit seemed to have long ago divided them. It didn't matter that the churches that rose above the tree tops would have been made of the same industry bricks that provided ground-level walls for the local taverns. The two groups met on separate days, read separate publications, and used similar words very differently—what was holy to the one was a term of cursing for the other.

Growing up there, I saw both establishments as club affairs. I had played guitar in a place called the Side Step Tavern one night with my best friend, Mitch, and then, after my dad left, Mitch invited me to his church. We would play music together in the youth group, and while I got to know some of the girls from school who went there a little better, I was moody and didn't really attract any new friends. Dad had left and made it clear I was the reason. I'm not just saying this out of the usual guilt kids feel when their parents break up. He really said this. He had told me a year earlier, when he picked me up at the library downtown.

"Your mother and I are arguing a lot," he said as I climbed in the car. "She wants me to spend more time with you."

Closing the car door, I went blank. I had nothing to say.

"You're causing a lot of strife."

After that, Dad did not spend more time with me. Then he left. I tried to become a guardian to my mom and my younger sister Emily, but that just caused more arguments with her over nothing. Emily didn't like me acting like I was her boss. That's how she said it, anyway.

When I hung out at Mitch's church, it went asserted in an unspoken way that moody kids had to be dealt with as a matter of testimony. It was clear that I should learn to carry on, like everyone else, as though both my parents were still at home.

I kept going to youth group anyway, partly because Mitch and I had put together a garage band that I valued more than he did. But he was also still willing to experiment. One Friday night, we found ourselves in possession of a pint of vodka and ended up not in a church parking lot but at Doc's where, I was told later, I engaged in the riotous spouting of rock slogans, quoting rocker Peter Townshend of The Who about anarchy. Doc was this college professor famous at our high school for his parties, and it was because of my high school that the cops were sometimes coming to his residence. It may not have been true, but I associated Doc with rock and roll, and that night the vodka helped me give voice to what I thought I knew. I was on my toes, bouncing to rhythms of the *Live at Leeds* tracks in my head, singing and reciting random parts of songs and shouting out into the backyard the famous lines from "My Generation."

My tirade explained my brief encounter the next Friday night Mitch and I ended up at Doc's again, parking at the end of a long line of cars that went back to the next block. Right after we got into Doc's, Mitch found out that Kim S. was there. In the car earlier, Kim S. had become his main topic of conversation. Songs we were learning to play and artists we were listening to now came second. Inside at Doc's, Mitch wandered to the back toward the patio, while I heard the Steve Miller Band playing on the stereo nearby in the living room. From behind, someone said, "So you like Pete Townshend."

I turned and saw this older guy, maybe 27, with short hair and an army jacket that was clearly from Goodwill because it had no medals.

"Yeah," I said. "I guess."

"Are you a seeker, then? Because that's what he is. A seeker. None of you kids give a damn about that."

I turned to the living room where the party was. The Steve Miller Band was not music for seekers. People were dancing and holding drinks, while the man in the army jacket continued staring at me as though he had just exposed a fake. It occurred to me that he had never been in Vietnam, but I didn't say anything. I never knew what to say about that. In our town, both sides had their supporters—both Vets and objectors. I walked away, slouching a little, pretending that I was carrying the sins of my high school on my shoulders. But then it hit me, and I started to laugh because that was the way older people talked to kids, and anyway what did Army Jacket Man without Medals know about a rock star he'd never met? I laughed because if I didn't then I might become too serious and say, Oh, I need to prove to you that I do know that Pete Townshend is a seeker. Here, look, I will now ruin all my relationships and become a seeker. I will leave friends, jobs where I'm comfortable, girls I really care about, towns I like living in, all to prove to you that I am a seeker. Is that enough for you?

I saw my glaring face reflected back in the glass of a liquor cabinet made of dark wood, and I looked around the living room for where the people dancing got their drinks. And then it really hit me and I started to think about Emily, my younger sister, and my mood went really dark. Dad had left because of me, and this was blackening everything around me then, and I left the living room depressed and went back to the patio and watched Mitch, among some of our classmates, talking to Kim S. She was smiling and laughing at him, and I still couldn't stop thinking that I should leave my family. It was because of me that my younger sister Emily was never going to know a complete family.

It is strange when I consider it now that the networks of family and friends we think will hold us and nurture us against choice and chaos are not, finally, as binding as the webs of our own making.

After getting confronted that night by the man in the army jacket without medals, I didn't leave my family. Instead, I stopped going to Mitch's church.

Keith, the drummer in our garage band, introduced us to a couple of his friends who wanted to join us, and suddenly the band got serious. This was when Mitch decided to quit, and he and our youth group friends faded into the background. As for the band, Jack, the drummer's friend, became our new keyboard player. He brought his friend in to be our new singer. Then they got us a gig playing at the River City Spring Arts Festival coming up in a couple of months. Jack and his friend had played there in another band a year before. In Jack's last high school year book photo, from two years before, he had been bearded, and with hair parted down the middle, he had looked like a member of Crosby, Stills, Nash, and Young. Now, his face was clean-shaven, his hair curly and styled, like he was ready to be on a different album cover in a band that regularly showered.

Cut loose into the company of questionable high school graduates three months before I became one, I moved over to play a bass that Jack owned. I found it easy to pick up, while Jack's guitarist friend became our lead guitarist. They had liked my guitar work, they told me, but because the other guitarist had played in front of people before and would know what to do, they gave him the lead. I'd played violin in junior high, and when I added it to our version of "All the Way from Memphis," Jack gave me attention. I belonged. Keith, our drummer and mutual friend, nodded. But I felt no connection. From where I stood, it was suddenly important not to fall for Jack's casual flattery.

In May, before the summer Festival, Jack got us a house party gig at the home of the quarterback of the varsity football team. His large basement opened out onto a pool area and a larger lawn beyond the pool. The backyard had been walled in.

We had been told to play just inside the sliding doors where we could be fully heard both outside on the back lawn and inside the basement. I started to get butterflies as we set up the drums and amps under a wall with a Schlitz Beer clock ad. After putting the PA system on the pool table, we turned on the sound and were testing it and tuning up when Emily and her friend came down the stairs and sat on one of the sofas pushed against the wall opposite the bar. I was suddenly having trouble with my face. Later I would tell Emily that I smiled at her for her to wave, but I really sort of smiled and then frowned and then focused on tuning my base because I didn't want anyone to see my butterflies. So I finally looked away from them while they watched us. Emily looked great, with her long brown hair curled around her shoulders. She was tall and slender, and younger than me by two years. I realized I was seeing her as a peer and not a little sister for the first time. Her blue eyes were large, outlined by mascara. As more people came in, she greeted them. I could tell already that she was going to be more popular than I had ever been.

Jack tested his microphone and watched Emily and Sarah from behind his keyboard, and I laughed—at nothing at all.

The crowd starting to gather was a mix of jocks and people I'd just seen in the hallways at school, all close now in the basement and gathered around the first keg. Our varsity quarterback was a junior that year, and he was throwing a graduation party for the senior players. There were balloons and banners, and chairs were pushed together to one side so that people could dance. Mark, the guitar player, struck a sharp bar chord to announce that we were on. We began our first set with the Blues, "Stormy Monday" and "The Weight," and by the time Jack and our lead singer launched out, two veterans sharing on vocals, I started to get a feel for my part. The singer chuckled and laughed and stroked his long hair as we introduced each song, and then he would wail on his parts.

Somewhere in the first or second song, I stopped being nervous and started riffing around what I knew. Then, Keith on drums kicked off two heavy versions of the Motown hits "My Girl" and "Tears of a Clown," and then slowed down with "Don't Worry, Baby." This was when our singer took over. He had quite a vocal range and was really very good at these.

After the Beach Boys song, a student from my class named Dan came up to us. He was in a white t-shirt, cuffed straight jeans, and his hair was greased back like he'd stepped out of the 1950s. With two of his greaser friends, he shouted "Rock around the Clock."

"That's our plan, friend," Jack said, "to party down all night." Keith, from behind, hit a few beats on the snare, imitated the beginning to what was all too familiar, and then Jack shouted out the first line to "Blue Suede Shoes," hitting the E chord on his keyboard. We broke out into an unrehearsed version it, and this brought in the *Happy Days* crowd. In the '50s nostalgia wave now, Dan was one of the guys in my class "coming out," greasing his hair back at a couple of dances and wearing t-shirts and cuffed high waters with white socks, finally getting his picture in the school paper. The whole thing seemed a return to something simpler I felt uncomfortable with. Aside from really liking and learning Chuck Berry, I felt that I was watching something that had already played out musically.

"Blue Suede Shoes" was easy, and we added our own frills to it, but it thrilled Dan and his friends as they danced haltingly in their costumes.

Finally, to finish the first set, Jack played the major seventh piano chord in eighth notes, the opening to "All the Way from Memphis." This brought the crowd fully to life as they danced around the pool table and around us, and I noticed they were even dancing around the pool outside. When we ended to huge cheers and applause, I knew Jack had been right about the order of songs. I got high fives for my few riffs on my violin. It surprised people. They knew to expect something, a sax solo, or maybe some thick guitar with fuzz. But I gave them the fiddle.

I stood outside with Emily and Sarah at the back door where a couple behind them was necking.

Emily's friend Sarah smiled at me. Her eyes were round and faded blue. The simple idea of talking to her because I liked her suddenly became complex, and I excused myself and went to the bathroom.

For the next set, as the sun was going down over the backyard, we got, as Jack announced, a little serious. First, Van Morrison's "Moon Dance," one of my favorites as far as playing the bass went. Then Jack's song "Under Deepened Skies," an upbeat love ballad.

During the next break, people wandered outside. On the other side of the pool, some of the football team had dragged a keg of beer onto the lawn and were doing challenges with it. In the shouting, I noticed that Jack had followed Emily outside, and the picture was this: Emily standing apart, turned away from Jack as he looked serious and focused on her. Someone told Jack loudly that Emily was only a sophomore.

We played two more sets. In the middle of the last one, we got word that he neighbor on the other side of the back fence had called the cops. Mist was floating into the darkness over the bright blue of the pool heated in the cold Michigan late spring air. Around the lounge chairs, half empty plastic cups and full ash trays left stains on the tables and chairs. It was after midnight, the hour when carriages turned back into pumpkins. We went acoustic, with our lead singer doing "Maggie May" and the Stones "Angie," and then Jack announced, "This is going out to a new friend." He began playing a nicely lyrical version of "Your Song." Then we turned the amps and PA off, and the electricity that had been underneath everything went quiet.

I sat down on the sofa to rest before we started to take down our equipment. As I did, the National Anthem started playing on the TV behind the small family bar, with shots of the flag fluttering interspersed with the Lincoln Memorial, the flag raising at Iwo Jima, an officer saluting a mourning widower, and the flights of jets. After the network signed off, Emily approached me from the dark corner where she had been sitting. I hadn't noticed her. Jack was right behind her. She stood there, watched me, and when I looked up I realized she was waiting for eye contact. Finally, she said, "You know what? I don't think you care about me."

This startled me.

"Sometimes, I just don't think you care what happens to me. I don't matter to you at all."

The next weekend, I woke up just after sunrise to pebbles hitting my screen and Emily whisper-calling at my window. I went out to the breezeway and let her in. She had stayed out most of the night with Jack.

"Emily," I said, "Jack is not like the Fonz."

Sitting on the lawn chair in the breezeway, she pulled her socks off. They were wet with dew. Her hair was tangled and curled. "I'm not looking for the Fonz. Everyone thinks I can't handle it."

"He's just playing you."

"Everyone seems to know more than I do."

"I know this guy. He's not right."

"I'm not even serious about him."

"I just want you to know. He's not a friend of mine. He treats me like a hired hand."

"I know," Emily said. "That's okay."

The next week, Emily came to our practices.

Mom made me send out graduation announcements. I signed envelopes and put my graduation picture in the cards sent to relatives. I was doing this when I heard a car pull into the driveway. The doorbell rang, and then I heard Jack at the door talking to Mom about taking both Emily and me out to Big Boys.

I put down the pen and gathered my stuff into a pile in the corner of the room and went with them. Jack's late sixties Buick smelled oddly of faint air freshener and something else that wasn't quite an outhouse and wasn't quite fresh. I sat in the back seat where a few Burger Chef wrappers on the floor seemed to have been there a while.

We drove down Plainfield.

"Are you getting the invitations done?" Em asked me.

"Sort of."

We passed the Big Boys.

"What's the deal?" I said.

We passed the tire center, a sewing machine store, and then the mall and headed out of town.

We went over the last bridge over the Oakwood River, the bridge that I had never liked going over. It had wooden rails far too shallow and weak to keep a car up, and the walk ways on each side were just a shallow step. It had been made a long time ago, and it went over the yellowed and darkened water of the river north of the city. Jack laughed and glanced over at Emily. "Does your brother get high?"

"I don't know," Emily said. She glanced back at me.

Jack said, "As your boss, I'm ordering you to try this. It will help your violin playing."

"What's wrong with my playing?"

He held out a rolled joint to Emily as we turned onto a two-lane blacktop. Jack glanced at Emily. "If you are going to do music right," he said, "you have to go down to your roots. You have to discover yourself." He poked the car cigarette lighter in and the orange-red heat began to circle around it in the dashboard.

"Right now our band is just starting," Jack said. "We're doing some blues, some Motown, some rock, some glam. But we need to focus. Who are we? We can be a jukebox for high school dances, play Grand Funk or the latest Stones. And that's okay. But who are we?"

Emily started to sing the chorus to "We're an American Band," furrowing her brow.

The lighter popped out.

Instead of Jack, Em reached for it, and as she held it up to the joint, I realized she'd done this already before. She drew hard on it, taking in a gulf of the smoke and holding it in and handing the joint to Jack.

The distinctive smell of contraband filled Jack's car, and with all the car windows open, I felt immediately paranoid. If a cop came up behind us, that would be that.

Jack seemed to be watching me through the rear view mirror. He took the joint, and drawing hard and holding the smoke in, he then handed it to me. I refused. He coughed and started to laugh. Em laughed with him.

And then Jack and Em were in a giggling contest in the front seat and saying "Oh wow" to each other, saying it louder and mocking each other every time they said it. I felt out of it.

The joint got shorter between them in the front seat, and I noticed that the sun was going down as we went over a shorter bridge and passed a farm. Jack looked out at the fields and flicked the last of the joint out the window.

"Awfully quiet back there," Jack said, checking me out in the rearview mirror. "Your brother is quiet."

"Some people live their whole lives like this," I said.

"Wow," Jack said. "You are a trip."

"I wrote a song," I said.

"A what? A song? Let's hear it."

I sang. "I see you standing on the ceiling/ but I am just reeling/ can't see how to get up from standing/ on the floor." I grew embarrassed and stopped.

We pulled up to a four way stop. Jack nodded. "It has potential. I'd have to hear more. Play it next time."

At the River City Fest, we played energetically. A big part of that energy came from me. It happened all at once. I knew my part, and I was not just comfortable before the large crowd. Suddenly, I understood that my bass was my one line of connection to the band, my family, and the few friends I'd had, and I played with new reckless power and meaning that the others noticed and responded to. We received two encores, and then we got off stage where a lot of people asked where we were playing next. We had fans. They were looking at me like I was someone new.

Mom came forward out of the crowd.

She stared at me. "What's wrong?" she asked.

I glanced over where Emily and Jack were arm in arm.

"I think I'm going to have to leave," I said.

"Why?"

"If you don't know, you don't know. I'm not welcome and I know it."

"You and your father just need to talk."

"That's never worked before."

That weekend, Emily went somewhere with Jack, and I didn't see her again. I was out with Keith, our drummer, tyring to play as fully as I could the role of the rock musician. I slept in his car at his place and got rides back to the River Fest to hear a couple of other bands. On Saturday night, I went home finally.

Monday morning came, and Emily still hadn't come back from River Fest or where ever she had been.

I sat strumming my electric guitar, which was hollow bodied and had cost me $78 three years before. It had three pickups. It was not a Fender or a Gibson, but I had been so captivated by the pickups and the price that I hadn't thought too much about that. And I hadn't noticed that the action on the fret board was too high. I would try leads, but they were difficult on my fingers, and I had to press harder than normal. When Mitch and I had played together, I would play through his small amp, and then I would hear how the different pickups on my guitar sounded. Otherwise, I would go back to the soft sound of my hollow bodied electric, which no one could hear coming from my bedroom, even with the door left open. Most nights over the last three years, I would play my hollow bodied guitar, and outside my room it probably sounded like a series of random, indeterminate clicks, sort of like those Search for Intelligent Life on Other Planets sound waves, where only the most expert will determine, no, someone is out there wanting us to listen. Mom would walk by my room and ask if I had done my homework.

Then it was Tuesday.

I still hadn't heard from the band, and Emily hadn't come home either. I started to feel unsteady about what I'd say when Jack came over or called a rehearsal. For a month now, Keith had been wanting to do a recording, and on Tuesday afternoon, he called me—I thought it would be about that. Instead he asked, "Have you seen Jack?"

"No," I said, "why would I see him?"

"Well, him and Emily."

At some point, I went out, and when I came back, I saw Mom waiting for me at the breezeway door.

She looked at me. "Do you know where Emily went after your concert? I know she was with that piano player. But where is she? I know there's no school, but she should be reporting in."

I shrugged. "I never approved of them being together in the first place. I tried to tell her."

I went to sleep that night, and woke up to Mom standing in the grayness of the hallway. My clock showed that it was about five fifteen in the morning. I sat up. She saw that I was awake and stepped forward, opened the door all the way.

She spoke in the last vestige of her normal voice. "The police just called. Emily is dead."

I felt something inside of me suddenly cut away. "This is reality, isn't it."

Her voice wavered. "A car accident. She and Jack are both dead. Your father is sick."

I swallowed. "How?"

"They found his car at the bottom of Oakwood River. Apparently it happened last night." She bowed and covered her face. "They just found it three hours ago."

It was summer, so there were no huge school assemblies with crying girls, no sudden appearances of strangers telling me they'd known Emily in a class.

The world of the grieving is a world seen mostly in hindsight. It is no help to offer the consolation that they have their memories to draw on, when their memories are where they tunnel day and night through darkness.

After both funerals, attended by hundreds of people, I sold my guitar and got fifty dollars for it. I wasn't sure which way I was going. I was a graduate and found myself in narrowed prospects, a trapped coal miner feeling around in the dark for a way out to daylight, tracing my steps back and forth over the last three months, from youth groups and Mitch to the gig we did for our high school on the night Emily confronted me, when the first fork in the road of my life appeared. I wanted to be back there, acting, choosing differently, standing up at the party and saying to Emily, "He's a good singer, but no, he's not worth it." I labored under the possibility that I could have done any number of things to change this outcome.

After the funeral, Dad came home again, defeated, shocked. We had denied the connections to each other, and now, too late, the one person we had loved we'd never see again. I was now living in the same place he was.

A few weeks went by, and I stashed my money and my few clothes that I had in the garage and waited until night. When asked, I said I was going out for a walk. I took my stuff from the garage and got out on the road, doing what I should have done the afternoon Dad told me that I was breaking up the family. It was a wrong gesture, a lost one, done out of time, like everything I did now.

I am still on that road. After miles and miles traveled and many more years, I still have not ventured far spiritually. The old stories of exodus or trying to get home capture this—the distances are longer in terms of years than they are in miles.

The Other Pictures

Waiting for the coffee to finish brewing, Jim Massad held his off-white coffee cup and looked at the backs of heads in the cubicles before him. Each had various personal items decorating it, each cubicle colorful and suggestive of worlds somewhere other than this place of dirty brown temporary walls inserted with tacks and staples and transparent tape and cream colored desk tops. Then there was his own, which, in addition to the standard office supplies, housed only an empty frame. Several days had passed, and though people had certainly walked by and looked at the empty frame, no one had commented on it or asked about it. This was probably just as well.

At the coffee station, Jim looked out the window at the street. He saw why people got tattoos. He wiped the smear from the edge of his cup. He had stood here so often getting coffee between documents and jobs, and again he looked at the campus street and thought of his cliché. Though it had always appeared to him like the gray skin of something asleep as it led up a shallow slope toward the arts and humanities building, now, suddenly, it seemed ordinary. The pebbles in the road, what his imagination was always converting into scales, now led him to think that he fantasized too much. He hadn't really been seeing the street for what it was. There were other fantasy pictures he had framed in his mind. Hemingway surfing the net—would a text message or a tweet work today as his "one true sentence"? Hemingway tweets would make a good marketing tool.

He filled his cup and then returned to a job description that had come that morning from Natural Sciences; he understood that this was how it was. He really was living a double life. Perhaps if he had put up the picture frame but left the picture of the model's photo the frame had come with inside it, people would have asked what he planned to put there. It might have led to some questions about his personal life. But he hadn't done that. He'd done what people didn't usually do. No one paid any attention until something was not done in the normal way, and then one had to be watched. He had worked too long in human resources at this larger religious college in town. Now in his late fifties, he never voiced objections, opinions, or even observations. Finally it reached him that his coworkers in the other cubicles, with less than two years of college, thought he had no observations to make at all.

Here he had looked out at the road for so long and entertained himself with his fantasy that the road could be a sleeping snake, when really it was just dead concrete. And that tree across the way really was blocking the horizon.

Beverly, in the next cubicle, began talking to Shannon in the cubicle next to hers. Shannon was having trouble with her husband, and Beverly, who had just gotten her hair done again, said, "Men and their needs. I just don't know."

Well, Jim thought. No one had noticed his empty picture frame either. He leaned back. Yes, he agreed silently with Beverly, men were stupid. Dull about the import of new hair styles and new blouses, they were focused on their sports and their sex needs. Perhaps, given the way men and women were, if we ever did discover life on some other planet, we would never be able to recognize it as life once we got there because we would assume that any life would be just like us.

He thought of his father and mother long ago. Their marriage had been a détente, an agreement of foreign powers worked out in the kitchen, the bedroom, and the lives of their children. Jim remembered sitting down to dinner, prepared by his mother, and his father demanding that she sit down with the rest of them even though she wasn't finished with some of her work in the kitchen.

He would order her to come and sit down. This was the worst it got, but Jim had silently decided he would never treat anyone that way.

He looked up from his empty frame there in front of him. Someone was printing invoices a few feet away, and the door opened and a student was walking in to make a request.

Most of his co-workers, mostly women, had inspirational writings around them, little keepsakes that said encouraging things as though addressed directly to them from God to keep them going. How much it took to get through the day without sensing the meaninglessness of it. It was a dream they were all in. Until now, he had found refuge in fantasizing that the road outside was a serpent.

Choices were made.

After he touched up the formatting to the Natural Sciences job announcement and added some boiler-plate text about diversity, disability, and workplace hierarchy, he hit save, attached it to an email for the Provost's office. Before he could question that this was really all he was good for, making sure that university documents being made public fit the standard, he stood and took his off white, stained coffee cup to the window where he decided to look at something other than the street. He didn't care that he might be cited for not working, or not adding to workplace productivity, or something the school had recently been cracking down on to meet the new budget demands. That tree across the road on the lawn was spread out big and broad and cut off his view of the horizon. The street was dead to him, but the tree there, well it blocked his view. The horizon was gone.

Laughter came from the back cubicles. It was from Caitlin, the new worker. When he was busy with his fantasy of the road, he had hardly noticed this about the tree and the horizon before. He glanced back at Caitlin's area, blocked by cubicle partitions. He looked out again at the tree spread out like a large, trunk-enforced dandelion gone to seed. He understood that a boundary had fallen across his life. He had come from the business world all those years ago to help people. He had said this to the alumni magazine when they hired him, before he had any vision of the office they would house him in. It was to his credit that he did not think it strange that he had never been considered material for management and had never been promoted.

"Hey, you can join us?"

Walking to his car after work, Jim was startled by the familiar voice from several rows down across the parking lot. He looked up to see Caitlin standing with the young man Jim had seen somewhere on campus before.

"I don't think you need me," he said. "I mean by the looks of things."

"Nonsense," Caitlin said. "You don't get out enough. I can tell."

Jim looked at Caitlin, then her friend. He wanted to ask, how could you tell that I don't get out much? Is it because I'm old? Maybe I do get out. Maybe you don't know.

In a Tai restaurant, they ordered drinks. Jacob, a younger man, from music, with a blonde tousle of receding hair and short side burns, was married, and he talked about the music department.

Suddenly, Caitlin said, "So, Jim is the only person in our office without pictures of his family. No pictures of wife or kids."

Jim smiled. "I have a picture frame."

"Is it empty?"

"Yes."

"Why would it be empty?"

Jim shrugged. "Because."

"Because what?"

"I don't have anyone." That came out as far too maudlin. "I'm single" would have been better.

"You never married?"

He was starting to feel cornered. He glanced over at the bar. "Once."

"What?" Caitlin said. "You need to explain."

He thought, for the first time in years, of how to explain Debbie to someone who had not met her, to explain her jagged, broken intensity, and their stormy two years together. Two years had almost seemed longer than he deserved with her.

"There isn't much to explain," he said.

"Yes there is. There always is."

"Well, twenty five years ago, my wife had a miscarriage. After that, we divorced, and then she remarried. There isn't much else to tell."

It was all factually true. Twenty five years before, Debbie, pregnant, had gone into a diabetic coma and lost their child. They had had a funeral for the unborn, had given her a grave marker, and then a few months later, Debbie had told him that she had decided to give him the chance to "someday have a child" with someone who wasn't going to have her problems with pregnancy. She left him, then, though she stayed in their apartment for a few months before finding one of her own. A year after letting her go, he learned that Debbie had remarried.

Every year, Jim returned alone to the grave of his still born daughter.

"Did you name her?" Caitlin asked.

"Angie."

"Did you know that Melissa, next to my cubicle, had a miscarriage?"

"No."

"Was it a diabetic reaction? Did she go into a coma?"

Jim suddenly respected Caitlyn. "Yes, that's what happened."

Jacob sucked on the ice in his rum and coke. Then he said that he and his wife were currently expecting, and that consumed the next ten minutes of their conversation.

Having shared his lone adult intimacy, Jim felt himself, as Jacob talked, fading again into background. He thought about Debbie again. She had been over-weight and had smoked also, and when they met she had been on the wagon for three years. She seemed stable, but then there was that occasional intensity, something broken from her past. She told him she loved him and seemed ready immediately to marry. That moment, when he decided to marry, reminded him of the arrogance with which he had later announced he was leaving insurance compensation over 20 years before to work for the religious college because he wanted to "help people and make his life mean something," as though this new job would automatically lead to new, meaningful adventure.

He finished his beer and glanced at Caitlin, fresh from campus life events, Caitlin who had lost her faith as a student at the school, where strangers from across the state were thrown together in dorms and had to share their life stories. Just like they were doing now, Jim thought. So simple. Surely, college amounted to something. It had taken him years before he had gotten over his own college experience and stopped referring to the small private school he had graduated from in the seventies, Charity College, as "highly accredited." Now, working at another private college, he realized that all private schools tried to seek for ways to look and sound elite. When he'd applied for his first jobs in the early eighties, he had often called Charity "highly accredited." When he was with Debbie, he would say that about the school. "Some of the people I knew there, most of them," he would tell Debbie, "were from out east." The truth was that as he thought about it now, he understood what once was and was not.

When he got home that night from the Tai restaurant, he checked his Facebook page, but it all seemed like empty space.

That night, he awoke from a dream. Caitlin was reciting from First John, "Dear children, keep yourselves from idols."

On Saturday, he went to his writer's group at the church. He had been going to it twice a month because casual conversation came easily enough, and he could talk about ideas. The others even liked the fantasy story he had written and thought he should do more with it. Each of the five of them had read enough of their work to each other to be comfortable. This Saturday, two of the regulars were missing, and after only two people shared, Millie, the retired school teacher, put her notepad in her purse and said,

"Well, I have things to do today. I'm going out tonight. I'm going dancing."

In the parking lot, talking to Vickie after Millie left, Jim said, "I'm afraid I've been living a double life."

Vickie laughed. "That's a great story line." When he didn't laugh also, she said, "Have you talked to Pastor about this? What kind of a double life?"

He glanced at the road leading out of the church parking lot. "Oh, there's the life of expectations and comfort. And then there's the real life. What's really happening."

Vickie seemed relieved. "I've often felt that."

"I'm afraid I've thrown my life away on the former."

In the week that had followed the happy hour he had shared with Caitlyn and Jacob, Jim had not taken the outing as an invitation to now approach her cubicle or to act as though they were friends, though Caitlin had said hello in a more familiar way and was the lone colleague to take note of his picture frame and pat him on the shoulder. This was noticed by the others around them, first Beverly and then Shannon, though he still kept his secret. Telling Caitlin about Angie, he had almost broken down a wall, though for the rest of the week it appeared to hold.

After the writers group on Saturday, he breathed the air as Vicki got in her car and drove away. It felt like it was time. He drove out to the hillside cemetery under the old oak trees where they had provided a grave for her, and he knelt down. All that had not come to be, all that never would be, these were not traces in the minds of the living. And so, in a way, was his life, all that others, the living had not noticed, traces of former hopes that would never be. He thought about coworkers with their pictures at work. It would be too much, but what if he were to bring more picture frames? One of the ways he had learned to cope early on was to recognize how much of our lives never took place, how much potential was always being ended. If he might place them around his desk, empty and propped up, they might ask to buy one, or take one. But they would never get it, and he would just be seen as more odd than before, as mocking them, or perhaps just losing his grip.

He glanced down at his daughter's grave. The stone read "Loved and missed." He had never been allowed to know her, except for Debbie's old words during the pregnancy about how different the child had been in her womb. Debbie had been pregnant before their marriage. She had had an accident in college, and this one had also ended in a miscarriage. But what she had been able to offer Jim was that their daughter had been very different, an individual, kicking her sides in a way that the earlier child never had. And Jim believed that God knew her as surely as He knew Jim. This was a person.

These were some of the same thoughts he always had when he came here. But now he looked across the green and shadowed hillside. Spring was full in the air now rather than fall. He saw things differently somehow. He felt his thoughts move away from the past and toward the future, as though his lost one were letting him go somehow. It was as though he didn't have to be responsible for this alone anymore.

There were these empty picture frames, and he couldn't get them out of his mind. If there could be one, then there could be many. And why not? But maybe there shouldn't be. Maybe that would be doing too much, cheapening what really was. Or wasn't. Or was.

It was something again to think about them.

He might bring the second frame in on Monday.

He might wait a week before he brought in a second.

Well, maybe two weeks. Maybe not at all. He'd have to see.

Veronica and the Slant of Light

I bowled my first 200 game with a Christian fellowship on campus.

I'm not a real bowler, and 200 isn't great to real bowlers. Even amateurs in Friday night bowling leagues might average 225. And I hit my 200 game just once.

Before my fiancée died almost two years ago, I did not go bowling with her, and before that, I had not bowled since I was about sixteen. But now, just about every Friday night, bowling has become one dignified part of my self-improvement program. Sort of an AA of my own making without the clichés. That's what I have turned it into, anyway. No one I'm bowling with knows that I'm doing this. They think we are just bowling. But when I get excited, they get excited, too, because after all we are Christians wanting to encourage each other. A few weeks ago, following my excitement over a 194 game, one of them suggested we start a team. He didn't really get it. It hasn't been the same for anyone else involved. To state things clearly, I am one of a few graduate students regularly attending the fellowship. None of the others is past twenty-two, and none has experienced the death of anyone other than a grandparent yet. They haven't faced the sudden, unexpected cutting away of someone who is supposed to be there, going on with you.

As for the whole team thing, certainly 200 is a far cry from the perfect 300. Yet for me, it was a personal best, and it was in my thoughts today as I sat in the auditorium off the main wing of the student center.

Today, facing the loneliness that comes with being a gradu-ate student waiting between requirements, I started to get into the part where the waiting brings me back around to the fact that I'm still in school, and this starts to feel like wasting my life. Sitting there, isolated, not sure of any promise beyond my classes, in the middle of the growing crowd waiting to hear a writer sponsored by both my department and the Education department, I noticed suddenly that the women around me, both peers and professors, talked only among themselves. The men, scattered about, had thick glasses that, when turned my way, seemed to reflect certain pages of text relevant to the occasion. Somewhere in all of this, my 200 game randomly came to me, and it was soothing, and I began to feel confident. As the rows of chairs filled up with more people, I even looked up. And I saw it, the light that slanted through the curtains, and I thought about Veronica.

We were here on Friday night, in the bowling alley down-stairs. Thinking about that, about Veronica and bowling, I looked past the cohort around me and instead reflected on the slant of light coming in through the long, pale green industrial curtains. We get this in February—all the strength the sun can give from a low point in a cloudless horizon, as though far away to the south it is spring. For now, there are long shadows here in the winter sunshine.

Attention shifted around me as the director of the University Writing Program came forward and applause charged through the audience. Here and there someone scooted a chair to get a bet-ter view. I checked my watch. The bleach in my jeans, after doing dishes in the group home last night, was still strong. I was going to have just enough time after hearing this author to get to work.

The director introduced the writer who, with more applause, came forward and arranged his papers on the podium, waited for the hall to fall silent. Then he began to read.

"I will show you into a child's country," he read. "But take warning. A child, you might have to remember, does not desire as a man does. No, a child will value the crudest stone, what a man would cast away. A child will make that stone live. But she can also let go when. . ."

How can I describe it? This language, though only an introduction, had aroused expectations, and suddenly the seconds on my watch seemed opened into the new space usually shrouded by the counting of tick, tick, tick, and I was taken out, just as I used to tumble out into the tide of Lake Michigan, toward new cold, shocking depth.

Yet as the writer continued to read, something far away from the image I had been drawn by took a distant shape, and suddenly I was looking around at the teachers. The linguistic tide had receded.

I waited through the story, heard other good lines, but it went on longer than I could stay, and finally I had to leave to meet Veronica outside. She was taking me to work today while my car was being fixed. I stood, passed the row of legs, conscious of the smell of bleach in my jeans, and in the aisle I walked to the back exit. Out the doors and onto the cement steps under the frozen sun, I saw, among the students passing by, college men holding hockey sticks.

I'd come back to State after mourning Sonia's death. I call her my fiancée, though it's true I hadn't yet proposed to her when she suddenly died. It was that now I wish I had proposed, and I said to people that I might as well have because we were that close. Now I am on the verge of finishing a Master's Degree. In a small, second-story apartment I found quickly last fall, I now look out daily at frozen streets where undergraduates walk by, most of them business or marketing majors. Someday, after all of their binge drinking and sex, they should return to families in smaller Michigan towns to work in middle management for their relatives' businesses. From my room window, I have a view on where they pass under the snow billowed on the trees, with cars going by where steam comes up through the manhole covers and makes spots where the dark pavement comes through the snow. The snow always makes it easy to think I really belong somewhere else. I can tell myself I am just here for the season. I am headed elsewhere.

On the steps of the student center, as I waited today, I thought about Veronica. Like me, she was raised Catholic. Her family was so Catholic that she was named after a saint. In fact, all but one of her five siblings had been given a saint's name, though today her parents are no longer Catholic. She told me all of that because she thought that everyone would think she was named after the girl in the Archie comics, whom she doesn't resemble at all. But she didn't need to tell me. I knew from Catholic tradition that Veronica was also the name of the woman who tried to help Jesus as he was being led to crucifixion by wiping the sweat from his face, and in doing so she removed her cloth to see the bloody imprint of the savior's face.

I knew that from the nuns who taught us.

I was grateful that Veronica had agreed to give me a ride to work. We had chatted one night last fall and then, late, started a board game. She was really good at Scrabble, and I was an English major and was supposed to be also, but she still won with small words strategically placed.

Then we sat in her kitchen because her roommates were out or asleep. She began to tell me about her heart condition. She had been born missing a heart valve, and her heart got really bad twelve years before when a new surgeon came through St. Louis and operated on her and she has been fine now. The heart surgeon was one of the life-changing miracles in her life.

I listened and was very thoughtful and we moved to the doorway and stood, and there were no words between us as she moved closer to me and I stayed where I was and our eye contact caused me not to notice the closeness or that our hands were touching. There were no words between us, and this might have been awkward ten years before, but then we were holding hands. And then we kissed. I heard the bowling pins crash down in a strike.

Today, on the drive out to the group home just outside of town, as I gave Veronica directions, I thought about how strong our kisses had been, but I was also thinking about the realism of what had happened. I admired her blonde, wavy hair and her large brown eyes made me think of the words, "A child is what I had to become." She wanted to work with kids. Our first talk, even before bowling, had been about teaching. We had a lot in common, and she was better at thinking through a teaching lesson than I was. And the truth was, I wasn't sure I wanted to work with young kids. We drove into the country, passing open fields, some with ravaged, skeletal rows of beaten corn stalks. Veronica asked me how the writer was. She had meant to see him, but she had already finished her degree last spring and didn't really technically belong anymore. I had thought about her during the reading but didn't tell her that. I told her about his opening and becoming a child again. After half an hour, when we reached the home, I climbed out of Veronica's car and thanked her but did not kiss her. I knew she didn't fully understand what had gone wrong with me before, but I wanted to tell her how mixed up I was and had been since losing Sonia. Instead, I said, "I want to talk to you tonight," and then turned and went down the driveway to the home. I'd tell her later.

The driveway wasn't shoveled and the old tire tracks had hardened. The blue van sat in the middle and I saw behind it a black Camaro.

I went in, passed the foyer to the steps leading up half a level to the main floor, and passed the office where I heard the voices of two co-workers. In the living room I sat down, and I recognized the voices belonged to Kurt and Martha, the other two scheduled for tonight.

Kurt, the proud owner of the Camaro, and Martha are both twenty-two. They are both probably smarter in the sense of knowing what is really going on than I was when I was twenty-two. At least they act as though they are smarter, though neither of them has finished more than a year of college. They never get my jokes. Martha has insight. Kurt talks to me as though everything about me is all on the surface. But Martha has recognized that I need some sort of healing, and to her credit this may be why she doesn't laugh when I tell my jokes.

As I sat there today, I heard them mention Kristin, another of our fellow workers, and then her pregnancy and coming marriage, and I thought I detected a sour note in it. However, since I wasn't part of the conversation, I let it wash over me and stood up.

I passed the office and stuck my head in to say hello, then went down the stairs to the foyer again and then down another half set of stairs to the door to the lower level, which is posted with two signs in large red and black letters, one reading, "CAUTION: DO NOT ENTER" and one the below it warning, "FIRE HAZARD: KEEP DOOR CLOSED." These signs make no sense. Beyond the door is where the residents spend all of their time. I suspect that the signs are there to mislead.

Through the door, the room is brightly lit, with windows looking out on the backyard, on the patio and swing set and then the broken stalks and husks of the garden under the snow beyond. Immediately in the room there are large, soft old chairs, a sofa with fat pillows, and a color TV. Next is the dining room and a counter with plastic toys over the fireplace. Then there is the kitchen. On the TV this afternoon a soap opera played to the empty chairs and sofa. I turned the soap opera off and went to the kitchen to start hot water for coffee.

When the residents came in through the CAUTION and FIRE HAZARD door this afternoon, they lined up listlessly under the Jesus picture-clock over the fireplace. It's one of those dreamy portraits where Jesus looks like a cross between a well-dressed collie and Sir Walter Raleigh. You expect him to start speaking in King James English, telling us to "suffer the little children." Under the picture this afternoon the residents, alive and breathing, waited to hang up their coats and put away their lunch pails as taught. I had the kitchen sink full of hot water and bleach.

At the front of the line, John Greer held a plastic bag with soiled jeans and underwear, and under his black beard, his mouth half-opened, he was wondering at me, swaying slightly. I smiled at him. He smiled then, reassured, and began to confidently hum the melody to the *Bonanza* TV show. I took his thermos and dunked it in the bleach water. Three of the residents are hepatitis B carriers, and the bleach disinfects everything. As I dunked John's spoon and fork, I saw the movement out of the corner of my eye and gently turned.

Standing at the end of the line, Bernard had just hit himself. With one eye narrowed and his tongue out and pointed, he squinted threateningly. Except for the tongue, it was a fair Clint Eastwood squint. Bernard has Down's syndrome. He is large boned, and his cheeks are prominent. His straight hair is combed to the side over his forehead. This afternoon lines were folded deeply under his eyes, and an open wound marred his face, a new sore on older scars. Even as I looked, he dug a gouge in his hand.

He saw me observing this. So he threw his lunch pail, open and clanking, to the floor. "This is your warning, Bernard," I said. I've been through this one enough. Months ago, on my first shift, Bernard had hurled his lunch pail to the floor, and in panic I had run from what I was doing to check on the floor to see how damaged it was. That had caused him to, as they say in this profession, escalate. He threw the kitchen chairs at the walls and then put his arm through the dining room window.

Today he stood, wavering almost, over his lunch pail, wavering over what to do next, over whether or not to destroy himself or fall placidly at my feet. It is amazing also that few of the other staff members know this about Bernard. They are scared, as I was, by his scars and his huge limbs.

I again absorbed his Clint Eastwood squint in my trained, bored nerves, showed him I was in synch with him, and I was with him.

He sighed, rested.

As though I were his understanding friend and had just forgiven everything he had done, I said, "Pick up your lunch pail, Bernard."

He squatted and picked it up. He brought it to the counter. I shook his hand and said, "Hang up your coat."

He walked to the cloak room, avoiding contact with the others.

Bernard is the challenge. Too much stimulation nauseates him, sets him off into self-abuse. Too little attention bores and angers him. He gets moody, cries and starts to abuse himself. It took me five months to figure this pattern out. He is a study. Behind his distorted, bearish appearance I have found the kind of awareness that I sometimes fancy most people must have. The trouble is that his person is revealed in direct proportion to the amount of his physical presence you are willing to take in at once, for he has no words to open your ears to him. Yet he has lived for a long time in there, and he likes to laugh with you, if you will. Like most people, he has his own reasons for being lonely.

This is what I had to learn in order to stay here, to keep this job, which, for all concerned, amounts to minimum-waged charity. And when I did, and that only after I learned about costly charity, I learned that Bernard's challenge wasn't too tall.

The other residents were still handing me their thermoses as Bernard came out of the cloak room and slugged himself in the face.

"Bernard," I said again, "this is your warning."

He did it again. He was having a terrible day.

I walked around the kitchen counter and took a chair from the dining room table and set it away from anything he might reach over and break. I pointed to it and said, "Five minutes." He sat down. The others moved away. He looked around, but everyone ignored him. He gave his Clint Eastwood squint again, but the next minute and a half passed without him abusing himself. Another minute and I would let him get up.

His squint has held my interest since I first read his case history in his logbook and learned that he hung around with his brothers a lot as a child, and the suspicion is that they abused him. He has hundreds of scars all over his body, some of them thick. The report doesn't say so, but I imagine his brothers taking him to see Clint Eastwood movies. Or, perhaps they went to the movies, and then when they got home they went around squinting and picking fights with each other. And, of course, they were Bernard's role models. This seems quite likely to me. I can imagine it.

As Bernard sat there and the squint relaxed and he breathed calmly, Bob stepped up and handed me his thermos. "Went school?" he said. "Drank Kool Aid?" Bob has echolalia, which means that, unlike Bernard, Bob has some ability for speech, though he is only able to echo the last phrases of sentences spoken to him. Bob, nevertheless, is handsome, with large blue eyes and healthy white teeth that form an overbite. In the cartoon version of all of this, he would be made to look like a rabbit. Here at the home someone on staff bought Bob colored underwear and a subscription to *Us* magazine. Every month, when Bob's magazine comes, it is placed in his hands and as he thumbs through it he says, "Rode bus? Rode bus, ooh gosh." Then he laughs and relaxes and says it again, turning the idea over as a memory. "Rode bus." After he thumbs through the magazine once, he leaves it somewhere—on the table, under the Jesus clock, or at the counter by the program logs. For a day or two it stays in the basement. Then it ends up in the staff bathroom. Staff must have a separate bathroom because of the hepatitis B infection.

With his three minutes in the chair expiring, I let Bernard stand up again and led him to his plastic rings, which he picked up and, as he sat down on the sofa in front of the television set, began to twirl. Walter, tall and drugged with an anti-seizure pill, staggered off to bed. John Greer came out onto the dining room floor and pointed at the ceiling and said, "Wha?" Then he began to hum the theme from *The Beverly Hillbillies*.

The fire hazard door opened.

Kurt and Martha came through.

"Summit House is coming over tonight," Martha said to me. She was in a black blouse with a black scarf collar, and she wore tightly fitting denim. "Hi guys." She waved to John.

I nodded. Summit House is the sister house down the road. Occasionally, the staff there brings the Summit residents over. Their residents are women, of course, all of them functioning at about the level that our men are.

Martha sat down at the dining room table with three black notebooks. Vicki, the home supervisor, does this when she works with the guys. Martha, when she works, has taken to doing the same thing. It is one more method she uses in her attempt to show the residents that she is in charge.

Kurt, a weight lifter, swayed and sat down across the table from Martha and opened his newspaper. "Didn't see your car out front," he said.

"A friend brought me."

"Friend, huh?" He looked at me. "Must be a pretty good friend to come out all this way."

John Greer came from the TV area grinning through his beard, looked over Kurt's shoulder and pointed. Then he began to hum *Bonanza*.

"So many people have quit here," Martha said. "In twelve months fourteen people have quit."

Kurt turned the page. "If the front office gave you any reason for staying, it might be different."

"Oh, I don't know," I said. "Maybe it wouldn't be any different."

"Fourteen people in twelve months," Martha said. "That's a serious turnover problem for a home this small."

"Are either of you thinking of quitting?" I asked.

"As soon as possible," Kurt said.

I thought of his Camaro payments and nodded, then asked Martha, "Are you?"

"It's terrible for the guys," Martha said, shaking her head and looking at me.

"Really," said Kurt. "No wonder Bernard has problems."

"Well, this is a hard job," I said. "I can't say I look forward to coming in. I'd as soon be home reading. Nobody pays you for that though."

Martha nodded.

"Once I get here, of course, I'm always drawn out of whatever was depressing me."

"They do bring you out of yourself," Martha said.

"So who's the friend that gave you a ride?" Kurt asked, turning the page again.

"A friend."

Kurt laughed.

"Her name is Veronica. Not named after the comic book character."

"What comic book character?" asked Martha.

"We were both raised Catholic. She's named after a saint. Which is probably why she gave me the ride today."

There was the sound of someone coming in the front door, then footsteps were heard on the stairs. The basement door opened and Kristin, short and thin in a white ski jacket and a knitted green cap came through. Of course, since being told that she was three months pregnant, I expect to see her, well, growing. But she didn't look pregnant today. She didn't return our greeting and walked into the laundry room. Martha pushed herself up from the table and followed her.

I said to John Greer, who still stood by us at the table, "I wrote a poem today."

John said, "Na? Na?"

"It goes like this." But then I couldn't remember.

John laughed. He pointed at the ceiling and hummed the theme from *Bonanza*. Kurt had gone back to his paper.

Meanwhile the door to the laundry room had been closed and muffled talking came through. This went on for five minutes.

Finally they came out and Kristin left as sullenly as she had come in.

Martha sat down again. She continued where she had left off in the black notebooks. "You did Bernard's sign language program?"

"Sunday night," I said.

"That's the last time anyone did it."

I stood up then. "I guess I'll get dinner ready."

"I hope he's in a better mood tonight," Kurt said, "with Summit House coming over."

"He's been bad this week?"

"A terror."

"You're his special friend," Martha said to me. "He counts on you." Martha pushed herself up again and walked toward where the guys were sitting around the television. She was going right for

Bernard. She touched him on the shoulder. This surprised him. He stamped his feet and his rings fell in his lap. He dug into his lap for them and then slugged himself in the stomach.

Martha had backed up onto the dining room floor.

"Bernard," Kurt yelled. "Settle down."

Bernard was standing up and slugging himself a second time.

"This is your warning," Kurt said.

Bernard gave the sign for music.

"In three minutes, if you settle down." Kurt was mad at him.

Bernard nodded and breathed deeply. Kurt helped him find his rings again and he sat down and started twirling them, though I noticed the Clint Eastwood squint twice.

"I just think that Bernard must have had brothers with dark hair," Martha said. "That's why he responds so well to guys."

"It didn't help me when I started. But maybe."

She smirked. Martha has clipped, black hair and round blue eyes. I can tell that they are honestly blue, too, because she doesn't wear contacts. Her main features, her straight nose, her chin and cheek bones, are well defined.

"I don't know," I said. "I guess I always feel like I'm sitting on dynamite when I come in here."

"I know it."

I unwrapped thawed hamburger meat and dumped it into the large frying pan.

"Who wants to dance?" Martha asked.

The house smelled of peanut butter cookies Martha had baked right after dinner. The dining room table had been pushed back. The women from Summit House sat on the hearth under the Jesus clock and on chairs. With the TV turned off, our residents looked blankly into the air.

No one answered Martha. On the radio an old Bee Gees' song, "Love is Such a Beautiful Thing," was playing, and Kurt strummed along on the house guitar.

Walter, now wide awake, had the house cat in his lap. He stood up and brought it to Janey, who sat on the hearth smelling her fingers. Walter set the cat in her lap. She yelled and threw the cat, sliding, under the dining room table, where it scrambled on the slippery floor and then scampered away.

"Janey is in a bad mood, Walter," Gina, her staff person, said.

Walter smiled. "D-yeah, Janey." Then he petted her greasy hair.

John walked up to Walter and forcefully sang the first line of the theme from *The Beverly Hillbillies*. Martha took his hand and began to dance with him. Bob walked across the floor and stood next to me biting his thumbnail and saying, "Rode bus. Rode bus," as though he were nervous about asking one of the girls out.

Walter put his arm around Janey. She let him do it. Gina, I noticed then, had been looking at me, but when I looked at her, she glanced away. I stood up and led Bernard, twirling rings and all, past everyone to the bathroom. "It's time to shave, Bernard," I said, and he lifted up the ends of his lips twice. This was a smile. It seemed that he had been ignoring everyone and instead blissing out with his twirling rings. In the bathroom, the razor buzzing, I gently ran it over his face, each movement smooth. Then I handed the razor to him and he shaved a stroke on each side of his face and then handed it back to me. "Aren't we old pals?" I said.

He nodded.

"I hope so," I said.

I began thinking about Veronica and our kisses, as pure and clear as any I had received. It hit me that Veronica was spending time with me and not just the whole group. What Kurt said about her giving me the ride hit home. I was a little older than everyone in our Bowlers Anonymous group, and I was taken in by the kiss. I had already suffered through a lot of self-inflicted pain and I wanted to spare Veronica, at twenty-four, of any of that. I had told her that on the ride out to the home that first night we had kissed. I was sort of warning her away.

My complications went back about ten years, to the blues band I joined before my high school graduation. I played the bass for them, and then one night Emily, my younger sister, came out with her friend from high school to hear us.

That was the night Jack chased Em. The following week, they went out. I had introduced them, and they were in a car accident that sent her forever away from us all.

Bernard and I walked back to the open floor and Martha gave Bernard a peanut butter cookie.

Then, without further introduction, Martha said, "Kristin went in for some tests."

At that moment I didn't know who Kristin was. Then I remembered. "Tests? For the army?"

"About her *fetus*."

"Oh."

"She wanted to make sure it was alright genetically."

"Aren't those harmful? I mean, to the *fetus*? I mean, I don't know, but. . ."

"And inaccurate," Kurt said. "I tried to warn her that they are inaccurate."

Martha looked at me with her beautiful eyes. "They told her that, based on the tests, the baby is deformed."

Kurt said, "Rob doesn't know it yet."

I had to ask. "Rob is her fiancé?"

"I told her the tests might be wrong," Kurt said.

"She just wants to get married," said Martha. "She doesn't know if she should tell him."

"She wants to marry a guy and she doesn't know if she can tell him?"

"Or get an abortion," Martha said. "I can understand. She's had a bad family life. Her parents divorced and all, and she just wants to be married, to get away from that. I can understand."

I glanced at the red second hand sweeping around the bottom half of the Jesus clock. Gina walked over and began to talk with Martha. John leaned in between them and said, "Nya? Nya?" He was very happy. This was a great night of fun and friends.

At ten p.m., with the girls from Summit House gone home and all our residents sleeping in their beds, Martha and Kurt went home. I got the observation log down from the shelf and sat at the table. I began writing my observations. I wrote about Bernard's self-abuse and the scars he had come home with in the afternoon. I wrote that he hadn't been shaved since Sunday. I wrote that everyone was happy with Summit House over. Then I found that I was thinking about when I was twenty-two. I had a part-time job. I drove a small van for adults like Bernard, Bob, Walter, John, and Janey, only I drove them home to their aged parents instead of to an institution. I remembered one fall overcast day pulling up to the curb in front of their day programming building, and I saw them all gathered under an old tree. In their faces, under their hats and scarves, was something I've known ever since that day. Right there, on the surface, were the features of disability. Another age would have used a different word, probably a word like "monstrosity." But I recognized that day that it was really the disabilities showing on their faces that made them human, and not the scarves, the hats, or the lunch pails with Spiderman, Snoopy, or Barbie they were clinging to. I saw in their various distortions who they were. I saw this only for an instant as they climbed in, courteously, one at a time.

This memory has stayed with me, including the families they were returning to, the care they were receiving, the identities they were holding.

I didn't write this in the log book. This was, after all, writing for the social sciences, not a humanities essay. I got up and did a quick bed check of everyone, and after that I sat where our guests had been dancing in the TV room just a couple of hours before and turned the lights off. And it occurred to me to pray. I prayed for Kristin and her *fetus*. I prayed for Bob, Bernard, and for me, because it appeared that I was being given a second chance also. Though the training period was long, I was about to be pushed forward.

And then I remembered what I'd said in the afternoon about talking to Veronica when I saw her again tonight. I would have to tell her. I had left my sister to die. Then later, I hadn't been honest with my girlfriend who should have been my fiancée, who had waited for me to propose. I wasn't about to hurt anyone again.

I glanced away and saw the moonlight falling along the floor in front of me, and I turned to the window and saw the moon for the first time. My 200 game came to me as something that wasn't perfect but wasn't bad either. The point was to keep on trying, and it hit me as the light came through the part in the curtain. Spring was coming. I stood and went to the window and looked out at how the moon lit the backyard where the swing set had been constructed for the men here who couldn't spell their names, and beyond it the fields, frozen again but with more of the fertile, promising ground exposed in the receding snow.

The Teacher who Bled Music

It was his first semester teaching part time there, and they had not given him an office. As he lived sixty miles away, he would walk across the campus yard to the mall after his late afternoon class let out at five thirty and wait there for his next class. The mall had been built recently next to the university. Few went there in the late afternoon, and his footsteps echoed on the hard floor. On the edge of the mostly empty downtown, the mall would close right at six in the evening anyway. It was the only mall he knew of that had been built right downtown where so many of the storefronts were now boarded up. It had been put there to draw business from the university. He wondered if it did better earlier in the day. He had begun to wonder why his first teaching assignment out of grad school had been here where the auto industry had recently abandoned the town to set up shop in Tennessee or Mexico. Tonight, he had been teaching just over four weeks and was starting to wonder what he was doing and if this would be all he would do. Then, tonight, the one student who sat in the middle of the classroom approached him. He'd hardly noticed her the first few weeks. She'd blended in with the rest pretty well.

"I know this is going to sound weird," she said. "Your teaching was like music tonight."

Several possible responses rushed through him, the most cynical the nearest the surface. He tried to avoid looking insecure, but he deeply wanted to ask her, Is that good?

Instead he asked, "You mean I rocked?"

"No."

He glanced down quickly, noticed she watched him, and nodded.

"I mean it was something else," she said. "I suppose this is just weird. But I think I began to understand something that you were saying about argument. I'd never quite seen argument in those terms you used before. I mean my dad always argues, and he always has to be right. So I never saw it as building bridges to the truth. Anyway, I will show you what I mean on Thursday."

On Thursday, their first drafts were due.

He found himself staring out the classroom window. He hadn't expected that—or anything. He hadn't expected anything. It came to her like music. Was there a teaching college for that? Could that be taught? Did anyone want it to be taught? Could one assess it?

"Your lesson was music to me." Could that be positive? Or a joke. Like those elementary school lessons on commas set to music.

Because of her comments, tonight he changed his destination, and instead of going inside the mall and getting a soft drink, he found his way outside where a walking bridge crossed over a small river that ran through the southeastern side of the city campus. Over the last four weeks, he had more often looked on the river from a distance, usually from his late afternoon class. But tonight he went there as a grayness fell over the once busy auto town, and he stood on the walking bridge and watched the water gently flowing underneath and thought about how he used to sing.

It came to him then, as he looked back at the building behind him now serving as a mall alongside the mostly vacated downtown strip, with the university behind him just up the street from the mall. It came to him that he inhabited a land that invoked transformation magically, all the time, like the good witch waving her star wand, like a teacher erasing a chalk board. He liked the image of a chalk board and not a dry marker white board, because the chalk stayed on the board. Evidence of the old remained and was background to the new figures written there. How much dust was there involved in this transformation magic? He himself was involved in one, a personal transformation, moving to teaching. And it wasn't all new ambiance and insight. Teaching the first class of the day sometimes left him feeling cynical. It left him feeling that in these times, post-factory, transformation had become the main industry.

Lots of gurus had set up shop, went to speak, rented halls, did filmed talks.

Water rustled below him, right near him. He wondered why he had stopped singing. He had studied writing also, and there was a point when he was doing both, playing in places where they heard him and also writing and reading poetry. He looked at the ripple in the dark water going under him. Now the students did not listen to him. It was as though he had become someone wholly different, as though in combing his hair differently for the classroom and dressing like a professional, he had lost the right to say what he had to say.

This was not an easy time of his life. Neither had his twenties been easy, he had to admit, when he was struggling to make a living playing in coffeehouses. When had anything ever been easy? There were just the right decisions that he felt good about in the middle of all the other stuff. Going to grad school had been the right move. It was strange to him now to be teaching people who were sometimes older than him who were also struggling because the plants had mostly closed and they were forced to find new work and they couldn't just graduate from school and go work in the plant for the rest of their lives. They counted their money—he could picture them doing so in their minds—and counting their chances and wondering what they could possibly bring to this new study they were taking. And why writing? Why was it required? Why was anything required? They had launched out for the new world and were now merely adrift.

He stood there above the water, glanced back at the college, thought about the class he had just left, where he had some eighteen year olds who hardly listened to him. In about twenty minutes, he would go in and teach the adults and they would engage him in conversations about life, and that would feel more welcome. A few years ago, he thought, when I was singing, and I wasn't that bad, and those eighteen year olds might have given me the time of day, maybe even listened to me. And then he thought that maybe his whole approach was wrong. And right there, on the bridge, he messed up his hair and parted it down the middle again. Like he was twenty again. He thought about letting his beard grow for three days. Really, he thought, I haven't really changed now, except that I'm not singing familiar songs to them; instead, I'm trying to teach them to write, part of the adult world they bounce off like astronauts on the atmosphere, seeing the colorful Earth and wanting to join it, but always coming in too hard and bouncing back out.

His student who had talked to him after class seemed not to be bouncing away.

Was this what came of a life of music after it was put away? Whatever he did afterward would be anticlimactic and mediocre, until, occasionally, the old life would bleed through.

"It came to me," she said, "like music."

Walking back into the building, he saw his shadow in the glass doors and his messed up hair, and he went to the rest room. He realized that it still mattered to him that music was still in the world. It mattered less that only a few heard it. Some heard it. It mattered that he could do this now. Instead of being an old, aging musician, he was a young teacher, and music still came through. He combed his hair in the new way before he headed back to meet his adult class.

Courtship in the Get-Away Car

———————————

Later, in September, Monica Dupree would finally view the on-line accounts of the August night she drove the getaway car—her car—from Rainbow Alley. By then, she and Winky would be in California, and though only a month would have passed, she would feel that the distance separating her from Michigan was much greater than that. She would have concluded that life was built on compromise, and she would then be viewing the film clips online of that night as a depiction that was not her. Sure, it was her car they used. But the online accounts made her into a girl trapped by a powerful cult personality.

The reality was so different. She was twenty-three. She had finished community college and had not gone on. Though she'd started to get interested in psychology her last year, it wasn't important enough to her yet to want to begin carrying a lot of debt. When Winky came back and started working at Gino's Pizza, she'd found him to be exactly her height, and she liked his muscular build and his ability to talk. She loved any man who could talk. He could talk about the news without it becoming a reason to think about building a bomb shelter and buying a generator, as it always did with her father. He could talk about his feelings, and she liked knowing where he stood. None of the online accounts captured this process behind their deepening involvement, and they didn't show how she and Winky had gotten out of Michigan and how she had almost immediately entered into a state of shock. That night, driving in the humid August darkness through Illinois, she tried talking about it.

"There was gunfire, Winky."

He said nothing.

"Did you expect that?" she asked. "The gunfire?"

He looked ahead, and she did too, into the bug-scattering path made by her headlights. She could see the shape of his face, his Errol Flynn nose, his mustache, his round shoulders full for his size.

"You were okay with it?"

"I just need you to drive right now," he said.

After that, he seemed to watch the darkened fields of corn that whipped by his open window. Pulling on his mustache, he would mumble something about deception, followed by sighing, and some version of, "Is that all it is?"

The third time he mumbled, Monica asked, "What? What are you talking about?" He wouldn't answer. All he had to do to make her feel okay about everything that had happened was talk. He didn't talk, though, even as the sunlight came the next morning and then turned cloudy as they crossed the Mississippi River into St. Louis. They drove by the famous Arch along the river. Monica wanted to stop and go up in it, but Winky suggested they keep going. It was the only thing he said.

An hour out of St. Louis, they had breakfast in a Hardee's, and Winky briefly came out of his silence.

"The problem of the partner remains," he said.

She stared at him. It was the Batman thing again. He was worried about his lack of dominance again, his too quiet super power. She put down her hash brown and tried to establish eye contact. "You have no partner problem, buddy. You have me. You're looking at her."

He was gazing up at the soda fountain set up for easy customer access.

"You think I'm joking?" she asked. The wrapper under her biscuit was greasy, and the full weight of the last fourteen hours came down on her shoulders. She was tired of driving but did not say anything.

They kept going through Missouri, and she had time to think that she may have misjudged his other interests. Back at Gino's, they had enjoyed what she would have called a strong understanding. When he'd gotten obsessive about the rapes that had happened in town and the movement of drugs, she hadn't thought about it much. Now, suddenly, on the long highway, she thought that she was wrong to have ignored this.

In the afternoon, in Kansas, they found a motel room. With some time before dinner, she suggested that they walk around a small shopping strip they had passed nearby on the way to their motel, and here they found the candy store. Back in Gino's, she had told Winky how in her grandfather's candy store, the smell of fruit candy and chocolates merged. Today, when she came across that same smell, it brought the memory of his store into the present. One didn't get this scent in grocery stores where the candy came in bags. One only met with it when the candy was in barrels and weighed by the pound. It was a small and stupid memory, she thought, but it was part of her past, and as they walked around the aisles, she realized that other than the smell of the candy, nothing was the same. This store was mostly of blonde wood, with a wooden floor, and it felt like a western theme, which wasn't like her grandfather's store at all.

They went back to their room and were hit again with the smell of old cigarette smoke. They'd asked for a non-smoking room. Winky held the bedspread to his nose and said, "They didn't even wash this. I could almost tell you the brand of cigarette that was smoked here."

"How could you do that? Have you smoked every brand?"

"No. Would I need to?"

"That's what Sherlock Holmes would have done. That's how he would know."

"He used science."

"Science and perception."

He put the cover down. "This smells like my mother's cigarettes, before she left. She smoked Kool's."

She studied him. "How old were you?"

"Young." He rubbed his face, lay back, and putting his hands behind his head, he crossed one leg over the other. "You know how after something happens, you can see everything in hindsight? You can see what you should have seen before?"

"Yes."

"You spend all your time dwelling on what you couldn't change anyway, because you really didn't see it clearly."

She leaned on him and rubbed his chest. "Can I ask you a question?"

"Yes."

"Why do you need a costume?"

He stared at her.

"I know, you needed one back in Michigan. But if you are subtle. . ." She looked into his blue eyes and his thin face, which reminded her a little of Errol Flynn. He was short, but he was muscular, surprisingly so, and had the body of a young wrestler.

"First things first," he said. "First, the partner."

"But if you have a costume, you really are asking for it," she said.

"How so?"

"A costume draws attention to the wearer. Any woman knows that. That's what surprised me about you. You are so quiet and subtle, and yet you wear the costume. Isn't that uncomfortable for you? And think of it this way. In a costume, you are, after all, making yourself a target. If you were Superman, that would be fine. No one could ever overpower you. They could pile an army and an elephant on you, and it would only work if they trapped you in an ambush of Kryptonite."

He smiled. "You had brothers."

"I told you I did."

"But that's proof to me."

This was almost normal again, she thought. "But for a man of normal strength, look what you do to yourself with a costume."

"What do I do to myself in a costume?"

"Really? Think about it. If you are a man of normal physical powers, you can be found and overcome. The costume simply anchors you in reality. Eventually, you will be located. But if you have no costume, and no one can pin on you an actual identity—"

"So how would my name be known?"

"Does a subtle man want that?"

"Subtle Man," he said, "not a subtle man."

"I mean," she said, "shouldn't a subtle man go unnoticed?"

She could tell that he wanted to correct her again. She said, "Since last night, they know you by the costume. I mean, yes, back there it made some sort of sense. You had to mask your true identity. But let's be honest, they knew it was you. But get rid of all that, and you are no longer a location. Technically, you are no longer anywhere."

"Well, you have been thinking."

She said, "The cool thing would be to leave a card. Or a silver bullet, like the Lone Ranger. Isn't that what it means to be subtle? Costumes are just sort of about branding. But you can do all of that on a business card. And it would be so much spookier to the bad people. A costume is too defined. No costume, and you are free of definition. You are free of detection. And to a perp, that could be terrifying. I mean, what does the FBI look like?"

He seemed to retreat back into the small compartment within where the dream held him. Rather than opening him up, she saw, she had instead added to his burden. She looked down at the stain on his shirt over his heart from salad dressing he had eaten that afternoon and then back up into his eyes.

He didn't say anything.

"You know what surprises me?" she asked.

He came back from his distance. "What?"

She said, "I am surprised that I've never heard you talking about the human potential movement—you know, 'believe in what you can be.' I mean this Subtle Man stuff sounds like the steroid version of that. You know, 'Believe in yourself.'"

He smiled. "That wouldn't be very subtle."

She paused. She stood up and faced the mirror. Her hair, which was curly blonde, seemed droopy. She needed a shower. She came back to the bed. A lot of women she knew wouldn't have come this far with this guy. She knew it. She rubbed his shoulders. "I believe in you, you know. I'm with you. I mean the gunfire, hey, that was just guns going off. They won't scare me away. I mean, I allowed you to use my car as your getaway car, didn't I, and it could have gotten shot up. But it didn't, but I didn't care. I mean I promise." Then she turned and sat on the bed. It did smell of cigarettes, and it was making her throat raspy. "But it would be nice to know that we are still the same way we were before." She looked into his eyes.

"I know, Monny," he said. "But things are always in flux. It's what I learned."

She found she was separating threads on the bedspread. One was red and the other was white, and she wanted them separated.

He reached over and placed a small paper bag of chocolate-covered peanuts next to her.

"When did you get those?"

"You told me it was your favorite in your grandfather's store." She shared two chocolate peanut clusters with him.

She was not like women who needed flowers and puffery, she had told him before, in Gino's. No gift could stand in for confidence, honesty, or time spent together. But as before with Winky, this gift had thought behind it.

Ahead, the mountains began to appear under the cloud front as she and Winky approached Denver, and Monica felt a shift happen. It was like air pressure, something forced in on them. Winky felt it, too, she thought. He stared pensively ahead, and she began to wonder in catastrophic terms again. Would they be caught? Would she have to sell her car at some point before they reached California? Would there be gangs when they got to California?

She felt the silence again. She wanted him to talk, and she glanced up at the mirror and pulled hair back out of her face.

Winky said, "My mother left us in Las Vegas."

"You said you were young. How old were you?"

"I was about ten."

"You know, we can skip Vegas, if you want. We can go south to Texas. It might be faster." She glanced at him. "Winky?"

He stared straight ahead.

She said, "I need to know where we stand."

He turned toward her on the seat. "I know. I know you do. Believe me. The chocolate peanuts were just a token. A small—"

"It was proof that you are still a player."

"A player?"

Maybe they were at the end of things. Maybe Gino's was their time. "Look, I've gotten chocolate peanuts before. Once I got a little thing of red jelly. On Valentine's Day. You want to be a player. Players need girls to play with. You want to bring me along with gifts. But I need you to talk to me. I need you to be my partner." She heard herself suddenly as a nag.

He stared ahead at the distant mountains.

No, he didn't hear it. Her small desire, it hadn't registered.

In Las Vegas, they drove down the strip to Circus Circus. They checked in, and she felt embraced and surrounded by all of the families in line to check in. The décor appeared to have come from the 1970s. It was clean, functional, and worn. In their room, as they were getting settled, Winky told her that he wanted to walk around the hotel and get a sense of it. This sounded off to Monica. "What," she asked, "are you going to walk the floors and look for open room doors?"

"No. You know there's a Circus floor here. It's fun. I just want to look at it again."

She suddenly thought of his being here in this hotel some twenty years ago with his mother, and she nodded and said she would stay back in their room. He left and she got out the motel stationary from the room they'd taken in Kansas. Looking out the window where she'd parted the curtains, she saw lower buildings and then desert beyond, and she played with a logo using her lipstick to form a red S. Then words came, and she took her pen and wrote, "Everyone must respect the police. But sometimes more is needed. We can feel it in our guts. At some point, only the one who can read between the lines can help. Call him the English major of crime. Call him subtle; he is the true hero who has enough understatement to smoke out the criminals in their roach nests and save the day. We need a subtle man."

To her, it read well. It could be a premise for a TV series. Reading her own words gave her confidence in her own convictions. This could help him to see her side of things. This would not solve absolutely everything. But it would put it out there. It was another option. He didn't have to see himself as a superhero seeking a sidekick; instead, they'd be partners. They'd be spies together.

It would also be fun to think of themselves as spies. Certainly more grown up than the superhero thing. Adult. Seductive, even. Deceptive.

When he came back to their room, he saw the red S she'd drawn and then read the copy she'd written. As he did most of the time, he sighed.

"Why does this trouble you, dear?"

"I don't want to be an enemy to the cops," he said.

"I didn't say that."

"You've just called them dense." Then the rest came out, everything she had heard before. He needed to be part of a super pair.

She thought of herself as his partner and told him so.

He simply shook his head. There had to be a Batman to his Robin, a Hulk to his Black Widow. He knew she wanted to be in on it, and he so appreciated her being with him.

She said that if he'd just recognize that the true nature of his enterprise involved her, he could be happy. This sounded a bit needy, but she was glad she said it.

He stared out the window at the sun going down.

She said "Isn't it okay for you, given your name, to completely rethink the whole superhero thing? I mean, doesn't each new hero come into heroism on his or her own terms? Sort of reinvent the old paradigm? That's what the good ones do. Or maybe, just maybe, you don't need to be a superhero. Maybe you—maybe we—are really spies."

He turned and frowned. "It's never something that we should rush."

"Rush what?" she asked. This didn't make sense to her, unless it meant he didn't want to rush finding his Batman.

"I don't need to rush. I have never believed in hurrying." He walked across the room to the door.

"Winky, I think—"

He raised his hand. "I think you do think. More than anyone I know." And he walked out.

The door had its empty metallic frame sound as it swung shut. The carpet absorbed the sound. Did he not want her? Did he not see her value? She wasn't worried about his leaving her. She was fairly certain that he wouldn't leave her here. But it was one thing when they were back home and they argued, and it was something else here.

She tried again to think from his perspective, as she had all along. This must be where his mother had left his family. What did that mean? Had that determined who he was now? She could sense that he really wasn't trusting her. Had the loss long ago determined and shaped all of this hero persona that was a shell around him? She had always rejected the idea that the past had power over the present and made people into who they were in spite of themselves. Winky's very existence challenged her on this point. Maybe this mother stuff did explain it all. Mothers, absent mothers, were powerful, overwhelming figures to their children.

She looked up at her purse on the desk. Winky was a bit older than her. He was probably done changing. If this was who he was now, how much difference could she make?

She got up and went to her purse. She picked it up. It felt too light, and she didn't hear the usual jostle of her keys. She opened it and dug for them under her wallet and her gum and her phone charger and tissue pack and her ChapStick and small makeup kit, knowing that the keys wouldn't be buried under those less used things. Her keys were missing. The side pocket of her purse still held her phone and the notepad from the Kansas motel they'd stayed at. But her keys were missing.

Winky had taken her car. The loss of her car was the weight that broke through her denial that he could be a psychotic or a conman. She had been lulled into giving up her car because of a bag of peanut clusters. That's probably how he would see it. But that also didn't make any sense, not in terms of the Winky she had known. The Winky she had known surely had to know that he wouldn't get very far with her car. He would know that she'd call the cops and he'd be pulled over and arrested for stealing it. Because that's what she was going to do.

Or maybe the knowing, rational Winky was the fake, the reasonable prop the conman Winky had convinced her to believe in.

She felt herself fighting the conman in her shoulders and her fists gripping her purse now as she went out, caught the elevator down to the lobby.

The wide open lounge of the hotel was full of families moving from the cafes to the games and shows upstairs where a lot seemed to be going on. There were so many families. She heard Danish or Norwegian as she passed an extended group, then a kid whining.

She went out to the parking garage and found her car under the lights where they had parked it on level 2. He had not moved it. She looked in every direction for him but knew that he wouldn't show himself like that. There was a paper on the dashboard under the wiper blade in front of the driver's seat. She took it from the dashboard and saw it was the red S she had drawn with her lipstick.

She looked across the full parking lot under the lights. In this moment, she saw her life divided into two paths, one turning back and going back to Michigan, and one following the road she'd called out to him but probably couldn't have: The road of the spy, Winky's partner.

To him, the S on the paper surely meant the superhero. But she had drawn it for herself.

Back inside the hotel, she was aware of how cheap it appeared. She had imagined luxury in Vegas, all that money could buy. But this seemed like it had been put up quickly.

She took the elevator to what Winky had called the circus level, where families wandered between rows of arcade games and a tightrope show of acrobats. In her mind, she pictured Winky's mother here.

In the rise and fall of applause, she made her way toward the crowd around a large boxed-in area where there were clowns stumbling and prat-falling around the margins below the graceful woman and two men on the tightrope and the swing up overhead. Monica recognized that the clowns were really acrobats also, just by the way they fell. In fact, it occurred to her, they may just be the most talented of this group, able to wear the handicaps of flat, large clown shoes, over- and under-sized clown suits, awkward purses, and tiny umbrellas while the others were swinging and flipping unencumbered through the air over the safety net.

The crowd seemed charmed by the faintly nostalgic, penny-free show, and the generosity expressed in this part of the hotel. She wondered, though, if Winky was even here. Her reading of his message on her dashboard—and it was a message—could be clearer. She backed away out of the crowd around the acrobats and moved across the corridor where a group of kids lined up in front of the arcade games to win stuffed animals. In front of one, two boys tossed rings over bottles, and behind the bottles were stuffed panda bears. She found herself next to a woman who seemed nervous as she looked both ways down the corridor and then in front of her at the two boys. A short man in dark glasses and trench coat reached up and stuck a paper with something red on it. The man wore clown shoes and a reddish-pink clown hair. Monica thought to move toward him, but he turned and disappeared in a crowd coming the other way. The two boys looked to be about ten and just younger, and the woman behind them checking her watch seemed to be connected to them.

Monica said to her, "Quite the set up here. Good place to take your family."

"Oh yes," the woman said quickly, without smiling. "They get the adults with the slot machines and the kids with the circus."

Monica frowned. "Has it been a good day?"

"Anything but." The woman glanced away at the trapeze show, seeming to want to direct Monica's gaze there, but Monica looked again on the right side of the bottle throw booth at the paper tacked up on the side, and staring at it, she recognized it as a photocopy of her logo she had made with lipstick. She glared back at the two boys and then turned to their mother, who had now moved away from Monica. She had backed up toward the center of the corridor where people were walking by her.

What happened next was confused. The woman turned to walk away and suddenly dropped to the floor. She shrieked and held her shoulder. Both boys heard the shriek, recognized it above the applause and the crowd, and turned around. The younger boy shouted, "Mom!" and ran to her, still gripping his rings, just as the figure behind the fallen woman shouted "help" and then moved away. Monica saw the clown shoes and the pink-reddish clown hair right beside where the woman lay holding her shoulder.

The younger boy held her good shoulder.

The older boy said, "Mom? Where were you going?"

Monica glanced around and saw the short man in the trench coat, now missing the clown hair and shoes moving toward a lounge farther down the corridor.

"Where is he?" the woman shrieked. "Did you see him? The bum tripped me. A clown. Where is he?"

Of course, Monica thought. Of course, nothing was resolved forever for the better now for this family. The woman had been prevented from using something pleasurable that her sons would for the rest of their lives associate with the abandonment. She might try again in another season. But there was also the possibility now that she could change.

As the casino detectives and the help moved in to assist the woman, Monica made her way toward a lounge where the short man in the trench coat had gone, where piano music could be heard and the deep voice of a full-throated woman finished what Monica suddenly recognized as an old Britney Spears song. Played at the slower tempo, reduced to the piano and voice, there was an appeal in it that Monica hadn't heard before. She made her way in and saw at a table near the front a small stack of papers. She saw the red S on the top one. She stopped where she was and took a seat in the middle, away from the door. She could see the way to the bathrooms.

There was a smattering of applause and then the singer said, "Got a request for an older song. First performed by Carly Simon for a James Bond film called 'The Spy Who Loved Me.'" And she began a piano chord that ran up and she sang the opening to "Nobody Does It Better."

At her table, Monica waited. Life, in her world, was built on compromise more than anything. The question came: For whom would they be spies? It was a work in progress, and she was thinking that the more you shared something, the more you learned about it.

Acknowledgements

Some of these stories first appeared in other venues. The author wishes to thank the editors of the following publications for first publishing them:

"Transistor Radio: A Story of Love and Technology" (2010) and "Directions from the Hive Mind," formerly "A Point of Saturation," (2011) first appeared in *Relief.*

"Lives of the Composers" (2014) was published in *Whistling Fire.*

"Side Step is Mainstream" appeared in *The Blue Moon Review* (1998) and *Mars Hill Review* (2002).

"When the Heart Plays Dead" (2012) was published in *Studio: A Journal of Christians Writing.* "Subtle Man Loses His Day Job" (2014) appeared in *Oddsville Press.*

"The Other Pictures" (2017) first appeared in *Broken Sky: An Anthology of 67 Press.*

"The Teacher Who Bled Music" (2019) originally appeared in *The Duck Lake Journal.*

"Veronica and the Slant of Light" first appeared as "Introductions" (1994) in a slightly different form in *Dreams and Visions #18.*